Rascal
DOES NOT DREAM
of
His First Love

Hajime
kamoshida

Illustration by
keji mizoguchi

Rascal

DOES NOT DREAM

of

His First

Love

Hajime Kamoshida

Illustration by
Keji Mizoguchi

New York

Rascal Does Not Dream of His First Love
Hajime Kamoshida

Translation by Andrew Cunningham
Cover art by Keji Mizoguchi

SEISHUN BUTA YARO WA HATSUKOI SHOJO NO YUME WO MINAI Vol. 7
©Hajime Kamoshida 2016
Edited by Dengeki Bunko
First published in Japan in 2016 by KADOKAWA CORPORATION, Tokyo.
English translation rights arranged with KADOKAWA CORPORATION, Tokyo through TUTTLE-MORI AGENCY, INC., Tokyo.

English translation © 2022 by Yen Press, LLC

Yen On
150 West 30th Street, 19th Floor
New York, NY 10001

Visit us at yenpress.com
facebook.com/yenpress
twitter.com/yenpress
yenpress.tumblr.com
instagram.com/yenpress

First Yen On Edition: April 2022

Library of Congress Cataloging-in-Publication Data
Names: Kamoshida, Hajime, 1978- author. | Mizoguchi, Keji, illustrator.
Title: Rascal does not dream of bunny girl senpai / Hajime Kamoshida ; illustration by Keji Mizoguchi.
Other titles: Seishun buta yarō. English
Description: New York, NY : Yen On, 2020. |
Contents: v. 1. Rascal does not dream of bunny girl senpai —
v. 2. Rascal does not dream of petite devil kohai —
v. 3. Rascal does not dream of logical witch —
v. 4. Rascal does not dream of siscon idol —
v. 5. Rascal does not dream of a sister home alone —
v. 6. Rascal does not dream of a dreaming girl —
v. 7. Rascal does not dream of his first love —
Identifiers: LCCN 2020004455 | ISBN 9781975399351 (v. 1 ; trade paperback) |
ISBN 9781975312541 (v. 2 ; trade paperback) | ISBN 9781975312565 (v. 3 ; trade paperback) |
ISBN 9781975312589 (v. 4 ; trade paperback) | ISBN 9781975312602 (v. 5 ; trade paperback) |
ISBN 9781975312626 (v. 6 ; trade paperback) | ISBN 9781975312640 (v. 7 ; trade paperback) |
Subjects: CYAC: Fantasy.
Classification: LCC PZ7.1.K218 Ras 2020 | DDC [Fic]—dc23
LC record available at https://lccn.loc.gov/2020004455

ISBNs: 978-1-9753-1264-0 (paperback)
978-1-9753-1265-7 (ebook)

1 3 5 7 9 10 8 6 4 2

LSC-C

Printed in the United States of America

The snow was really coming down.

Chapter 1

A Gray and Desolate Landscape

1

Sakuta Azusagawa couldn't comprehend what the doctor was saying.

"We did everything we could. My condolences."

He wasn't having trouble hearing or making out what the doctor had said. The fortysomething man who'd emerged from the operating room spoke clearly and in the silence of the hospital, even hushed voices sounded loud.

"What...did you...?"

His voice rasped. The question had just slipped out.

But the man in the green surgical scrubs did not respond. He wasn't even talking to Sakuta.

No, the doctor's focus was fully on a woman in an expensive suit who had long hair and seemed to be in her forties. Sakuta could see the resemblance she shared with a girl a year above him in school. His girlfriend. The one who mattered more to him than anyone: Mai Sakurajima.

More accurately, Mai looked like the woman in the suit—Mai's mother. Sakuta had met her once before. The fact that he'd remembered her face from that one meeting showed how much they looked alike.

"Then my d...Mai...she's really..."

Words fell from her lips one at a time, her eyes glued to the doctor's face.

"By the time she reached us, it was already too late."

He bowed deeply.

Sakuta simply couldn't process any of this. He knew the doctor was speaking Japanese, but nothing he said made any sense. His heart and body refused to understand, to accept the truth.

All sound gradually faded away. The only thing he could hear was the rushing in his ears. The doctor was still talking, but nothing he said reached Sakuta.

His ears were howling. Cut off from the world, Sakuta was struck by a sudden sense of vertigo. He'd lost his center and couldn't tell forward from backward, up from down. Trying to get a hold of himself, he fixed his eyes on a single point ahead.

Then a hot, searing pain ran across his cheek.

The stinging sensation brought his mind back to the present. He thought he heard the lingering echo of a crack.

"Bring her back!"

A voice twisted with rage shrieked at him. He could see a gut-wrenching pain in those eyes. She hadn't shed a single tear, but Sakuta could still tell.

A second and third crack echoed down the hall. Only then did he realize that the pain had come from someone slapping him across the face.

"…Give Mai baaaack!"

One more slap.

Sakuta didn't have it in him to dodge. He let her blows land where they may.

"Please, calm down."

Doctors and nurses stepped in to pull Mai's mother away.

"Give her back! Give my daughter back to me!"

Her wails stabbed into him like knives. He could taste blood. It wasn't his imagination—the slap had broken his lip.

A nurse spotted the injury and put a hand on his shoulder. "Let's get that looked at," she said. She gave him a gentle push, clearly suggesting he shouldn't be here.

He didn't have it in him to fight that, either. He obediently went along, moving like a sleepwalker.

"Bring Mai back! Bring her baaaaack!"

The sounds of a mother's grief echoed in his wake.

Sakuta was alone in an outpatient waiting room, his lip patched up.

"......"

He sat on the first seat of a five-seat bench.

The lights were out, and the only illumination came from the green of the exit sign.

This room was usually only used if there were so many people waiting to be seen that they ran out of chairs, but it was the middle of the night, well outside of normal visiting hours. The silence reminded him of that time he'd sneaked into school after dark.

Then that silence was broken by footsteps.

Someone was rushing down the hall.

And breathing heavily.

In moments, they would reach Sakuta.

Spotting her blond hair bouncing in a familiar side ponytail, Sakuta recognized Nodoka Toyohama right away.

She worked as an idol singer and had been performing a Christmas concert. She must have come straight from the venue without even removing her stage makeup. Or her costume—he could see it glittering under her coat.

When Sakuta looked up, her eyes locked on him.

"Sakuta...?!"

The footsteps stopped. Her face was tense, scared. She shot him a pleading look, like she was hoping against hope.

Sakuta realized instantly what she wanted and deliberately looked away. Nodoka's hopes would not be answered. And he didn't want to watch.

"......"

"Sakuta...?" Her voice rasped.

He said nothing. There was nothing he could say.

"Please, Sakuta…"

Her hand was on his shoulder, shaking him.

"Talk to me!"

She shook him harder.

"Why aren't you saying anything?!"

"……"

"Tell me why!"

He just couldn't bring himself to. And that was all the confirmation Nodoka needed.

"…This can't be real." Her voice trembled. "Not this…"

"……"

"Tell me it isn't true!"

His heart fluttered in the silence.

Sakuta forced his parched throat to life.

"The doctor said…when she reached the hospital, it was already too late."

Those words hadn't made any sense. They still didn't. He was just repeating meaningless sounds.

"…Don't."

Her voice sank like air was rushing out of her.

"That's…what the doctor said."

"Don't!"

"I really…don't know what it meant."

"My sister's really…?!"

Her hands were on both his shoulders, shaking him again.

"……"

"There must be some mistake!"

"……"

"Sakuta!"

"……"

"It's a mistake. It has to be. Tell me it is!"

When he finally lifted his head, Nodoka's tears were flowing. Her face was all twisted up from crying.

"Someone called my name," he said.

Nodoka sniffed.

"Then I was on the ground."

"......"

"And Mai was lying next to me."

He sounded almost delirious. His mind wasn't functioning at all. He couldn't think. The words came out unbidden like some broken speaker, describing what he'd seen with no comprehension of what had happened to him.

"The snow."

"......"

"It turned red."

"......"

At this hour, nothing in this hospital would prevent him from talking.

"Red all around Mai."

No matter how slowly he spoke, how fragmented, no one was hurrying him.

Nodoka was just listening through her tears.

"Only around her."

"......"

"I spoke, but she didn't answer."

"......"

"Mai wouldn't say anything. Even when I called her name."

The fear of that moment came rushing back, and Sakuta started shivering. The room wasn't cold, but his body felt frozen.

"The ambulance came and we rode in it, but Mai never spoke. Never moved. She wasn't...breathing."

Sakuta had prayed they'd reach the hospital soon. That was all he could do. Hoping if they did, the doctors could save her. He'd believed they would. Had to. Not a doubt in his mind.

"Why..." A whisper escaped Nodoka's lips.

"......"

"Why..."

"......"

"Why didn't you protect her?"

Teary eyes glared at him.

"Why didn't you protect Mai?"

"……"

"Why…why…"

"I…"

"Why didn't you make her happy?"

"?!"

He choked back the words trying to come out. Her outburst left his mind blank. He wasn't even sure what he'd been about to say.

"Why…whyyy?"

Nodoka collapsed to the floor, sobbing. She no longer had the strength to do anything but cry.

She started to topple all the way over but caught herself, her hand braced against Sakuta's knee.

"Why…"

She slapped his knee.

"Why…"

Then punched it.

"Why, why, why?!"

Over and over. He felt no pain. Her blows were too weak and carried no real strength behind them. Each one was weaker than the last.

"Why…why…?"

Her voice faded, too. Soon he could barely make it out.

"Sorry. I…"

But the words he meant to say vanished before they could be heard. The last shred of reason he held onto stopped him.

I should have died instead.

It would be easy to say that.

But Sakuta couldn't.

His body physically rejected the very idea.

Sakuta was here because of Mai.

He continued to exist because of her.

He was alive because of what she'd done.

How could he possibly say anything to diminish that?

So he choked back the rising bile, clenching his teeth until the rancid wave of emotion washed through him. He knew full well those feelings would never go away. There was no salvation to be found, no matter where he turned.

All he could do was wait for time to pass.

There was nothing else left.

That was the only part of this he understood.

He had no memories of walking anywhere.

It was anyone's guess what time he'd left the hospital.

But before the sun rose, he was outside his apartment, taking the key out of his pocket, and opening the door.

"I'm home…," he said out of habit. His voice was dry and hoarse. It echoed through the silent interior.

There was no answer. He lived with his sister, Kaede, but she was staying with their grandparents at the moment.

"……"

But as Sakuta took his shoes off, he waited for a response. He had hoped there would be one. For the last month, someone else had been living with them…and he'd gotten used to having her around.

"……"

He waited, but no answer came. He couldn't hear any slippers padding down the hall. Nobody came to greet him at the door.

That open smile was no longer here.

"…Oh. Right, it wouldn't be…"

It finally dawned on him.

The accident should have taken Sakuta's life. Once he was pronounced brain-dead, his heart would have been donated to little Shouko. The transplant she needed. Big Shouko's ticket to a future. But Sakuta was here, alive.

It wasn't just Mai's future that was lost. Little Shouko had lost her one shot at a transplant surgery…so how could the future version of her still be here?

"……"

The hole in his chest opened wider. The yawning void was eating away at him.

"…What the…?"

He knelt down at the entrance, feeling like he couldn't breathe. He instinctively clutched his chest, and when he did, something there didn't feel right.

"……?"

This felt *wrong*. Different from the day before. He touched his chest again, and it was definitely not the same.

"……"

Driven by doubt, Sakuta slipped a finger inside his collar and peered down his shirt front.

"……!"

The sight made him stiffen. The change was clear, and it rattled him. A wave of alarm rushed from head to toe.

"…Oh. I was right."

On one level, it added up. Of course this would happen.

The three claw marks running from his right shoulder to his left side…

…were completely gone.

Not "healed" or "faded." There wasn't a trace of them left, like they'd never existed in the first place. Just unbroken skin from top to bottom.

And the sight of this change dashed the one remaining faint hope Sakuta had left.

The absence of scars proved big Shouko was no longer around. It was real to him now. Perhaps there was still a small chance that little Shouko would get her heart transplant. But big Shouko had made it because she received Sakuta's heart—so she no longer existed. All those times she'd saved him…and now she was gone. She no longer existed in this world, or the world to come. The missing scars proved it. Sakuta's continued existence proved it.

"I couldn't…"

He couldn't protect anything. It was all gone.

"…This is a dream, right?"

That murmur slipped out of him.

The sights his eyes registered, the sounds his ears heard, the sensations his skin felt, the thoughts running through his brain—none of them felt real. None of them seemed convincing. He couldn't believe any of it.

He wanted this to be a dream. That was the only way this made any sense. A reality this harsh and inescapable *had* to be a nightmare.

When he woke up in the morning, none of this would have happened. That was the only way things would make sense.

Sakuta clung to that idea. In that moment, at least, it seemed far more believable.

2

The next thing he knew, the sky in the west was red. The cold of night was about to swallow the last of the sun.

The red of the sunset mingled with the black of night, and when Sakuta glanced up at it from the window, it looked like the end of the world.

"That might be preferable…"

He hadn't spoken in hours, and the sound of his own voice reminded him that he was still here. He couldn't remember what he'd been doing. Had he been sleeping? Just sitting still? Everything since he'd arrived home was a blank.

He was on the floor, and there was something in his lap. A tricolored cat. Nasuno. He could feel her warmth and the softness of her fur. The parts of him touching Nasuno were the only parts that felt real.

Their eyes met. Nasuno meowed.

She was probably asking for food, since she hadn't been fed since yesterday.

Sakuta tried to get up but felt woozy. He grabbed the *kotatsu* for support and barely managed to avoid falling. He must have been sitting completely still for a long time. All his joints hurt.

He didn't seem to have much strength left. Like Nasuno, Sakuta hadn't eaten for at least a day. He was dehydrated, and his whole body felt sluggish, like he was running a mild fever.

Sakuta carefully let go of the *kotatsu* and stood up. Nasuno was rubbing against his feet, and he headed for the kitchen to answer her demand.

He got the bag of dry cat food out of the cabinet and poured some into Nasuno's bowl. The portion size was a little bigger than usual. Nasuno peeled herself off his feet and started eating.

Sakuta stroked her back. The fur was soft. He could feel her warmth against his palm. But that was all it was. There was no comfort for him here. He didn't feel drawn to the tender sensation the way he normally would on any other winter day.

It didn't reach his heart at all.

There was a void in his chest, and he was numb to the world.

Nothing but emptiness floating inside. Sakuta wasn't even sure that sensation belonged to him.

He petted the cat for a while and after some time, he heard a noise outside. The intercom rang.

His body didn't react at all. Instead, Nasuno stopped eating and looked up.

"...It isn't locked," said a voice in the distance. No, it most likely wasn't that far away. He couldn't tell exactly. And he honestly didn't care.

"Kunimi, we can't just go in—"

"Sakuta! You here? I'm coming in."

He could hear two sets of footsteps. One was stomping down the hall and the other was following at a light trot. They came down the short hallway into the living room.

"Sakuta."

"Azusagawa…"

His guests found him kneeling next to Nasuno, and both called his name. He'd heard their voices somewhere before. They seemed familiar.

He looked up blearily. Two people were standing over him. A tall boy, Yuuma Kunimi, and a short girl with glasses, Rio Futaba.

They were his friends.

Yuuma took one look at him and seemed momentarily relieved. This was soon replaced with an expression of grief. Like he was barely keeping it together.

"What's wrong?" Sakuta asked. Unfocused.

"…We saw the news. About the accident," Rio said.

"We've been worried. Tried calling you all day," Yuuma added.

"Oh."

He looked at the phone, and the light was flashing on the answering machine. There were messages waiting.

Nasuno decided these visitors weren't very interesting and went back to her food. Sakuta stood up and went over to the phone.

He pressed the button next to the flashing light.

"You have four messages," the phone announced in very professional tones.

The first had been left that morning, at 7:03. It was from his father. (Naturally, they still didn't live together.) He spoke calmly, merely saying that he'd seen the news and was worried. Sakuta could hear Kaede talking in the background, demanding a chance to say something.

Their father must have handed her the phone.

"Sakuta, it's not true, right? This can't happen… Not to Mai!"

Kaede was all choked up. It was obvious she still hadn't accepted the news. She kept talking until the emotions overwhelmed her. Words failed her, and she dissolved into tears. Sobbing and sniffling, like a child throwing a tantrum.

After a minute, his father took the phone back.

"Sakuta, if you get this message, call us back. Doesn't matter what you say, just let us hear from you. We'll be waiting."

He hung up. His father never once asked if he was okay. He knew full well Sakuta wasn't. His father wasn't one to ask pointless questions.

The second message was left at 10:11. From Rio.

"Azusagawa, where are you?" she asked, clearly stifling her emotions. "Kunimi and I are worried. We'll come over later."

The third was a minute later, from Yuuma.

"Sakuta? I know Futaba just called, but we're coming, so let us know if you need anything. If you wanna talk for any reason, don't wait—gimme a call."

The fourth call was that afternoon. The time said 2:32.

He recognized this voice, too. It was a first-year student from his school who worked at the same restaurant he did: Tomoe Koga.

"It's Koga. Senpai…you can talk to me. I dunno if I'll be much help, but…I can listen."

The more she talked, the less steady her voice was. Her concern was plain as day. He could tell she was trying not to cry.

"I'll call again. Let's talk then if you're feeling up to it."

Her nose sounded stuffed by the end of her message.

"Messages concluded," the answering machine said.

A deathly silence settled over the living room.

Sakuta had been staring fixedly at the button this whole time. He pressed it again. There were only four messages, but the machine's history had logged a lot more calls. Ten in all. Half from his father's number. The rest from Rio and Yuuma.

"Sorry," he said. "I've been making you all worry about me."

He hadn't consciously decided to say that. His heart wasn't in it. It was simply an automated response to the situation at hand.

Yuuma grabbed his arm with a firm grip.

"Stop being stupid. Come on."

He pulled Sakuta toward the door.

"Come where?"

"There's a ton of photos and videos of the accident online," Rio said. "You're in a lot of them."

"Oh."

Sakuta sounded convinced, but his mind didn't follow. No matter what they said, his heart did not respond, and he made no effort to think.

"Everyone's saying Sakurajima was on a date with her boyfriend when it happened," Yuuma growled, glaring at the floor in open anger. "They're blaming you for it."

"For the time being, you're staying with me, Azusagawa. The media will be swarming this place in no time." Rio wasn't taking no for an answer.

"……Okay."

Once again, he responded without any real understanding.

He just didn't have the energy to argue.

Sakuta had completely lost all capacity to think for himself or disagree.

He just went with whatever seemed easiest and let the chips fall where they may.

"But I should call Kaede and Koga back…"

The last remaining thread of consciousness drew those words out of him.

"I'll talk to Koga," Yuuma said.

He put his phone to his ear. She must have picked up right away.

"Koga, it's Kunimi. Yeah, I'm at his place. Don't worry, he's with us. Mm."

He moved away, talking.

Rio was loading Nasuno into a cat carrier. She packed up the bag of cat food and Nasuno's dish, too.

When that was done, she said, "I'll be in your room," and vanished without waiting for an answer.

A few minutes later, she came back with a tote bag stuffed with spare clothes.

Rio had stayed here awhile over summer, so she seemed to have a good grasp on where everything was.

"Call your family on the move," Yuuma said, hanging up. He pocketed the phone and picked up Nasuno's cage and the plastic bag filled with cat stuff. "Let's go."

He gave Sakuta a nudge in the direction of the door. Sakuta followed like someone was pulling his strings.

They put their shoes on while Rio checked that all the windows were shut and locked. She took the door key from Sakuta, and he and Yuuma went out into the hall ahead of her.

The skies were dark.

Night was already here.

3

When they got to Rio's house, she'd said, "Don't worry, my parents won't be home till after New Year's."

True to her word, the next few days, there was no sign of either one.

Her father worked at the university hospital, so he had a room rented nearby to crash at. Her mother ran an apparel shop that worked with a lot of overseas brands, and she was often away on trips to Europe, laying in stock.

This mean Sakuta could stay at Rio's without worrying what anyone thought. He'd spent the time in a daze.

The one thing he had managed to accomplish was that call to his dad and Kaede. He'd let them know where he was and warned them that things could get ugly around their apartment, and Kaede should stay with their grandparents for the time being. Rio had been standing by, reminding him what he needed to say.

And they'd taken his word for it.

It turned out that his friends' fears were justified as the next day, there were a number of news vans parked outside his place. Yuuma had gone to check.

"This could last a few weeks," he'd said when he came by to check on Sakuta.

Sakuta was in a corner of Rio's enormous living room, listening like this was someone else's problem. He was on the carpet by the windows, gazing absently through the glass. He'd spent most of his time here since his arrival. It seemed pointless to sit anywhere else.

He didn't know when he was sleeping and when he was awake. He might not have slept at all. He was just staring into space, occasionally reacting to external stimuli. In those brief moments, the remaining shreds of his mind and consciousness allowed him to regain some notion of identity, to remember his own name.

The rest of the time was spent as if in a dream, trapped in a world of fiction where everyone else knew how to play their roles. Sakuta alone sat on the sidelines, doing nothing.

None of it felt real. There was no part of this world that could possibly be real.

Rio didn't try to cheer him up. She never laid any false platitudes on him. She just said ordinary, everyday things.

"Azusagawa, what do you want for lunch?"

"Bath's ready. You go first."

"Maybe you should lie down for a while."

"Sounds like the weather's going to be nice tomorrow."

Even if he didn't respond, her attitude never changed. She never once got annoyed and simply tried to be there for him.

And she took on the least pleasant task.

The night of the twenty-seventh. After dinner.

"Her wake was tonight apparently. Family only," Rio said, looking grim. "There's a service at a funeral home in the city tomorrow."

"……"

He didn't manage a response. His shoulders may have twitched slightly.

"The school's bussing us all there."

"……"

"I'm going with Kunimi."

"......"

She hesitated. "You coming?" she asked. She thought it was important for him to think about this, no matter how hard it was for her to say.

"I... No."

It had been so long since he'd spoken, it didn't sound like the words came from him. The voice was robotic, containing no trace of emotion.

"Okay. Sounds like a lot of work colleagues'll be there. Which means tons of cameras, so..."

That wasn't why he'd said no. He figured Rio knew that. But she offered a different explanation precisely because she *did* understand. She carefully tiptoed around the real reason.

"But you—," she began. Then she broke off. "No, never mind."

"......"

"......"

For a while, she stood next to him, not saying anything.

December 28. The morning of Mai's funeral service. It was cold and cloudy. Layer after layer of thin clouds blocked out the sun.

Yuuma came to pick up Rio just after noon, in uniform. Rio was wearing hers, too. Sakuta was used to seeing them in those outfits, but it felt wrong. Probably because despite all of this, Sakuta remembered that it was winter vacation.

"Um, Azusagawa...," Rio said before she left.

"......"

In the end, she decided not to finish her thought. Same as last night. The only difference was that this time she hesitantly tried again.

"Azusagawa..."

Sakuta spoke up, cutting her off.

"Take care."

He chose a phrase that made it clear he wasn't coming. He spat the

words out, like he was covering his ears, intent on not hearing anything else she might say.

"Okay," Yuuma simply replied. He and Rio walked away.

Sakuta watched them go, feeling slightly relieved.

When they were out of sight, he closed the door. Then he promptly
went back to his spot in the living room.

"......"

Sakuta knew what Rio had been trying to say. His heart was slowly
starting to work again. The more time passed, the more the real world
was trying to call him back. That was why he could tell what Rio had
left unspoken.

You should say good-bye.

Something like that anyway.

Even thinking those words was like a nasty screech piercing his
brain. It was physically revolting. His blood seemed like it was boiling. He couldn't breathe. He could feel his bile rising as something ate
away at him from the inside.

Sakuta raised his voice in denial. "I don't wanna...!"

He screamed to protect himself.

"Why the hell would I?!"

Rejecting the very idea helped him stave off the emotions that
threatened to overwhelm him. He crouched down defensively and
curled in on himself, retreating further into his shell.

He pulled in his shoulders, back, neck, and knees. Even his fingers
were balled up. They were so tight his fists hurt. His nails dug into his
palms, leaving red marks.

This was the only way he could withstand the anguish crashing into
him. He stayed like that, enduring, until the moment passed. Seconds,
minutes, maybe hours.

An unintelligible groan seeped from his throat.

"I should have..."

...died in that accident.

He got halfway through the thought when a female voice interrupted.

"This is where her funeral's being held."

Not a loud voice. Soft, like a conversation in a library.

The speaker was on the TV in the living room. Nasuno was playing with the remote on the table.

"Stop..."

Sakuta snatched it away from her. His finger moved to the green button, trying to switch the TV off, but...he didn't press it. Couldn't.

The girl he wanted to see more than anything else was on the screen.

"On this rainy afternoon, crowds are flocking to Mai Sakurajima's funeral service."

As the reporter spoke, the camera showed Mai's mother holding her memorial photo. Sakuta's eyes locked on Mai's face.

There were countless flowers already placed on the stand. White ones. He didn't know what they were called.

The camera pulled back, showing the whole venue. The space was big, but it was already packed tight with row after row of mourners. It looked like thousands had shown up.

A man in a funeral suit stepped up before the stand. A famous movie director, one even Sakuta recognized on sight.

His voice quivering, he began reading a memorial speech.

"Mai Sakurajima. Mai—I can call your name, but you'll never turn toward me with a smile anymore. We parted, looking forward to the next time we would be working together, and it pains me more than I can express that this is how we meet again. You were just six years old when we first met. Even then, you were already an actress. I'll never forget it."

He kept breaking off, fighting back his emotions. He was well into his sixties, but his voice was choked with tears. By the time his speech ended, they were streaming down his face. He didn't want to say good-bye. Every part of him made that clear.

And it wasn't just the director.

The entire hall was overwhelmed with grief at this unexpected, all-too-soon loss. There was no solace to be found. That much was obvious, even through the TV screen.

The next speech was from a veteran actress, one who'd played Mai's mother on a morning soap back when Mai was still a kid. By the time she reached the mic, she was already sobbing, and delivering any coherent remarks at that point was well beyond her.

Her costars came running in to support her. Everyone was crying, saying their good-byes to Mai.

Sakuta watched it like it was a movie.

Trying to convince himself it was just something happening on the other side of the screen that had nothing to do with him.

After broadcasting the service live for a while, the TV cut back to the studio.

The anchor was a man in his forties, solemnly watching over the broadcast on a monitor. Next to him was a woman serving as coanchor and a row of cultural commentators and former politicians, all watching in silence, at a loss for words.

The anchor sighed softly. The camera caught a hint of tears in his eyes. He took a long breath, turned toward the cameras, and began to speak.

"I'm sure the majority of you are already aware, but four days ago, on December twenty-fourth, Mai Sakurajima passed away in a tragic accident. She'd been acting since early childhood and was still only eighteen years old."

The coanchor took over.

"Mai Sakurajima first came to fame on the morning drama *Kokonoe*. She won praise for her acting talent and went on to appear in many movies and TV shows. I'm sure all our viewers knew her."

"She was a household name," a man on the panel agreed.

"She certainly was," the coanchor said with a nod At this point, Sakuta finally recognized her as Fumika Nanjou, a reporter he'd met several times before. She normally wore much brighter colors, but she was wearing a dark-blue suit for the occasion. "As our coverage of the service has confirmed without a doubt, she was adored by her industry peers and fans alike."

"Very true," the anchor said. "I actually met with Mai for a different program during the shooting of her final film in the days before the accident. The filming took place in Kanazawa, Ishikawa Prefecture..."

He paused, looking up and blinking several times. Then he put his fingers to his eyes, as if fighting something back. Sensing Fumika's eyes on him, he said, "I'm okay," and recovered.

"My apologies. She was really...such a sweet young girl," he continued. "While that footage was filmed for a different program, we thought we'd change those plans and show it to you now, along with highlights from Mai Sakurajima's career. If you would?"

With that signal, the screen went black.

Then it faded in on a scene from the morning soap that had introduced the world to Mai Sakurajima. She was only six, grinning from ear to ear. Playing a precocious kid who regularly eclipsed the adults around her. Impish but never annoying—people couldn't help but love her for it.

In interviews from her child-actress heyday, she always answered questions from adult interviewers with a poise you'd never expect from someone still in elementary school. There'd been a poll asking mothers which child actors they most wanted as their kid, and Mai had come in first by a landslide. When they asked her about it, Mai had joked, "Now I really can't do anything naughty." The adults all laughed.

The next clip was a big jump forward.

It was several years later, and Mai was in junior high now. Her face had matured, leaving no trace of the child actress behind.

The scene was from a horror film Sakuta had seen before. She played a mysterious, fragile girl. Footage from the making-of showed the director saying, "She can smile with just her eyes."

It was true—in scene after scene, Mai could captivate the audience with her gaze alone. This film had launched the second phase of Mai's career.

These were snapshots of Mai's life from a time before Sakuta had ever met her. Back when he only knew her as the famous actress Mai Sakurajima.

Other clips covered how she'd started working as a fashion model, and the first photobook she'd released had sold like wildfire.

And then she'd shocked the world by announcing a hiatus.

Only returning to work this year.

She'd tackled TV shows, movies, commercials, model work—and everyone had thought it was only a taste of what lay ahead.

As the narration wrapped up, they began playing footage of Mai filmed only a few days prior. It opened with her open expressions of delight at being reunited with some Kanazawa citizens she'd met on location.

"Oh, Mai! I didn't think we'd see you again so soon!" said the portly woman running the tea shop. She had a warm, friendly smile.

"I know!" Mai said. She then offered an explanation that threw a little shade at the man with her. "Usually, we film these things closer to the film's release, making it a nice little trip down memory lane—but here we are, not even a month later."

"Sorry," the man said. He was the anchor from the news. "We were told this was the only gap in your schedule—and of course, our staff leaped at the opportunity."

Without missing a beat, he said the production staff were responsible for the somewhat awkward timing. Mai and the anchor got ready for the teahouse shoot.

Scenes like that would usually not survive the final edit, but today, they were using everything. There was even footage of them discussing who should sit where. This showed Mai in her natural state, with a genuine smile.

When they finally did sit, they were facing each other.

"Did you come here regularly during filming?"

"At least three times a week."

"That often?"

"The director's got a major sweet tooth. He really liked the green tea *anmitsu* here but was too self-conscious to come alone, so he always invited me along. Pretending like he was just keeping me company." She laughed happily. "So I got him to pick up the tab."

"Speaking of sweets, it looks like they've got a number of treats for us today."

The portly woman served up the famous green tea *anmitsu*. Mai's was the regular size, but the anchor got the kind of bowl usually reserved for ramen.

When he looked shocked, Mai said, "That's the plus-size one. The director's favorite."

They began eating, talking as they did.

"It's been several months since you returned to work—does anything feel different this time?"

"I think I'm more willing and able to enjoy each job on its own merits."

"Were you not enjoying it before?"

"I didn't mean— You know I did! I just wasn't able to relax and have fun like I am now. I was putting too much pressure on myself."

Mai thought about this for a minute.

"I suppose enough time has passed. The real reason I was so stressed out then was because I was constantly fighting with my mother, who was also my manager. I'm grateful to her now. It was her hard work that got me all those opportunities and let me meet so many amazing people."

"And your mother?"

"I'm not about to admit it to her face, so...this'll have to do," she said, deliberately turning to the camera.

"We'll see what our director thinks," the anchor said with a laugh. "Speaking of your newfound relaxation..."

"Yes?"

"Do you think you're enjoying work more because of anything new in your life?"

"....?"

That was a leading question, and Mai glared at him. But he was conveniently looking elsewhere as he broached the topic.

"I mean, what else could it be? You know what I mean, right?" he asked, almost winking. "Of course it's that very special someone!"

Mai bowed her head, suddenly very formal. "I certainly caused a lot of problems for everyone," she said. The news of her boyfriend had caused a media frenzy. The anchor's show had covered it in great detail.

"You can't blame us for doing our job," the anchor said.

"No, of course not," Mai assured him. Her smile was polite and not much else.

Normally, that would have been the end of that topic. Few people could pry further when faced with the prospect of Mai's wrath.

But this anchor was not so easily daunted.

"Do you think having someone like that has changed you?" he asked.

Instead of evading the question, Mai admitted, "I feel like it's actually caused more problems."

"Oh? How so?"

"I said as much during the press conference. This is all new territory for me, so…I'm never sure of myself."

"Really? Mai, I *know* you've got him wrapped around your finger."

"You have some very strange ideas about me."

"You're a terrific actress, you're even more beautiful in person—I think I'm hardly alone in assuming you have this boy right where you want him."

"Well, I do."

"I thought so!"

"But I think I'm the one madly in love here."

She said this like it was nothing…and blushed a moment later.

"Wha—?"

The anchor almost did a spit take but turned it into a cough at the last moment.

Mai recovered her composure and leaned back into her chair. As if remembering the cameras, she turned toward them.

"You definitely have to use this," she said. Likely to the director sitting off-screen.

This smile of hers was genuine.

A smile full of life.

And with that, the screen faded to white.

Nothing but white.

The words **In memoriam** appeared, and then the screen went blank.

As black as if Sakuta had turned the TV off.

Then a crying face came on-screen.

Not an actor.

Not a cut to a commercial.

The TV remained dark.

He knew the face looking back at him.

How could he not?

It was Sakuta's reflection.

Tears flowing from both eyes, down his cheeks…

Quietly dripping into his lap.

He hadn't shed a tear after the accident, at the hospital, or when he'd heard the results of her surgery. Not a single one after Mai's mother went after him, or when he heard Nodoka's sobs. Even when he was alone, Sakuta hadn't cried. He hadn't been able to.

Four days had passed, and it was only hitting him now.

Only now did it catch up with him.

Seeing Mai acting so normal forced him to face the truth. He had no choice but to admit how precious those moments were—and how he would never have them ever again.

He finally had to acknowledge what he'd been refusing to accept.

——*"We did everything we could. My condolences."*

He'd known from the moment the doctor said those words. That knowledge had been inside him all along. He'd been well aware of what had been trying to claw its way out.

He knew what it was called.

Sakuta knew.

Everybody knew.

Every person alive knew.

This was grief.

It was slowly rising up, confronting him.

He'd tried not to see it, but it was reaching out and threatening to engulf him.

So Sakuta screamed out loud.

"Go away!"

He leaped to his feet and turned away. Covered his ears to block it out. That wasn't enough. He ran out of the living room and into the hall, almost taking a tumble in the entryway, but then got his shoes on and was out the door.

He didn't dare face this grief. He couldn't even admit it existed. Dealing with it head-on was out of the question.

Acknowledging it would mean admitting Mai was dead. By denying his grief existed, Sakuta was trying to refute the fact of Mai's demise. To will her death out of existence.

He had to run.

As far as he could, away from Rio's house, out of her neighborhood.

There was still snow left on the edges of the road.

The snow that had fallen that day.

That stirred up memories of the accident and sent a storm barreling through his chest.

A wordless rasp escaped him.

He brushed aside his tears and ran on, trying to leave his grief behind.

His breath ragged.

His lungs screaming.

His feet almost gave out.

But Sakuta just kept running as fast as he could.

If the grief caught up to him, it would all be over.

If it grabbed ahold of him, then Mai was gone forever.

That single belief drove him onward.

As long as he didn't accept her death, then Mai still lived.

That's what he wanted to think.

More than anything, he wished for that to be true.

Clinging to that delusion was all he had left. There was no other option. He had to do what he could to protect it.

But he knew none of that was real.

Because he knew better, he had to deny it.

Because he knew better, he had to run.

The sand grabbed his feet and knocked him down. The beach caught him gently.

He didn't remember anything about the run. But he knew these waves and the salty smell and the sea breeze.

When he opened his eyes, he was on the beach at Shichirigahama.

He'd walked this beach with Mai. Seen it out the window every day. So many memories in these sands.

"……"

The tears he'd fought off were flowing again.

He had to get away, but he was too tired to stand. Too worn out. He was gasping for air. It didn't seem to be getting better.

He was pathetically, horribly sad.

"…Help," he croaked. His voice was filled with raw emotion. "Somebody, anybody…"

He was shivering in the cold. It was the end of December, and the sea breeze was chilling him to the bone. He was wearing only his gym tracksuit. Far too thin to protect him from the elements.

"Somebody, save Mai!"

Oblivious to the cold, Sakuta was yelling at the ocean.

"Please!"

Begging.

"Save her!"

Hitting it with everything he felt.

"I'll do anything! Just save Mai! Save her! Please…please!"

But nobody answered. No one came.

"Save her... Help her... I'm begging you..."

He knew nobody could grant this wish.

But it was all he could do.

"I'll...I'll do anything! Just bring Mai back to me!"

Grief had caught up with Sakuta, and now it was smothering him. He was being pulled deeper and deeper into a whirlpool of darkness, crushing his very heart.

He had lost everything. Sakuta could feel himself shattering.

Wrung out.

Only a husk remained.

No light of hope.

Despair was all he could see.

It wasn't long before he couldn't even see that.

But he could hear one sound.

Footsteps on the sand.

They came closer and stopped in front of him.

"Stand up, Sakuta," a gentle voice called.

"......"

At first, he didn't believe his ears.

"Saving Mai is your task."

This couldn't be real.

"You know I'm right."

It couldn't be. This wasn't happening.

But his unconscious mind knew the truth, and despite his fatigue, he lifted his head.

Her dress fluttering in the breeze.

Her warm smile.

"...How?"

The breeze snatched his whisper away.

"How are you here, Shouko?"

He didn't get it. It didn't make sense, but his whole body was trembling. Not from the cold or from the grief. But because big Shouko was

here. That simple fact had him shaking with joy. The tears started flowing again.

"Oh! You haven't heard yet."

"Heard what…?"

For little Shouko to survive her condition, she *had* to have a transplant. But Sakuta was supposed to be the donor—and he hadn't died. He'd assumed that doomed Shouko's future, too…but here she was in front of him. She still existed.

"This here…" she said, putting her hands on her chest like she was cradling something precious, "…is Mai's heart."

"?!"

"It wasn't announced officially, but…the day of Mai's accident, by sheer chance…she became my donor."

"…Mai is your…"

"Yes."

"She had a card, too?"

"She did." Shouko nodded.

"B-but then…the future changed?"

Originally, it had been Sakuta's heart.

"……"

This, Shouko didn't answer. He didn't think she could. If this Shouko existed because of Mai's heart, then she was a different Shouko from the one who'd received Sakuta's and had led a different life.

Could he even call them the same person? But before he could ask, Shouko dropped a bombshell.

"Come. We've gotta save Mai."

"…Come…where?"

"Obviously—to the past!"

"……We—"

Before he could say "can't," she said, "We can."

She looked him right in his eye.

"Who is it you're talking to, Sakuta?"

Of course she thought that was funny. She was totally right, of course. Shouko being here at all proved time travel was possible in some form. Her presence proved what she said was real.

"Don't worry. Leave this to me."

She held out her hand, looking like she'd just thought of the best prank ever.

Sakuta shook his head.

Then he stood up on his own power.

"That's my Sakuta!"

He wiped his tears.

"Now come with me," Shouko said.

Her smile seemed thoroughly satisfied.

4

He had a lot of questions for Shouko.

Or he felt like he should.

But when he tried to put them into words, nothing came out.

"……"

Unable to break the silence, he just kept his eyes locked on Shouko's back.

They walked along the sands of Shichirigahama for several minutes. Then Shouko moved away from the surf and up a staircase. He followed her up onto the coastal road, Route 134.

She pressed the walk button, and they waited for the light to change. Cars were flowing in both directions, from Fujisawa and Kamakura, in equal numbers. The traffic whizzed past the two of them.

At last, the light turned green. Shouko started walking, so Sakuta followed. Three steps behind.

"Mind if I stop at the store?" Shouko asked, already turning toward the entrance. Sakuta waited outside, and she was back out a minute later, plastic bag in hand.

From there, they followed a gentle upward slope and crossed a single track.

"Here we are," Shouko said, looking up at a big building.

"......"

Sakuta stopped with her, the same sight reflected in his eyes. One he saw nearly every day.

They were outside Sakuta's school, by the front gates of Minegahara High.

"Hokay!" Shouko said. Sakuta just stood there while she put her back into it and pushed the gate open.

She got it far enough for a person to fit through, then said, "Come on," and stepped onto the school grounds, like she was doing nothing wrong.

"......"

Unable to bring himself to stop her, he followed after.

"Don't worry—it'll be fine."

"......"

"Mai's service is today, so the school's empty."

He hadn't asked, but she answered anyway.

"And if anyone does see us, well—you're a student here! And I'm an alum. Us being here isn't a problem."

She sure seemed confident.

Shouko made it sound like she'd take the Minegahara entrance exam, attend high school here, and eventually graduate. But that was all in the future. None of it had happened yet.

If someone caught them, and she blabbed any of that, it would only make her seem extra fishy.

He was sure Shouko was well aware of that, but she didn't seem at all hesitant. She looked straight ahead, making a beeline toward her objective. He still had no clue where they were going. But after a minute, it became clear their destination was inside the school building.

They went around the building to reach the yard; then Shouko opened the science lab window from the outside and climbed inside. Rio had told him about the window with the broken lock once before.

Carrying their shoes, they headed down the empty halls.

The lights were out.

Some light seeped in from outdoors, but the glow of the red bulb above the fire alarm seemed unnaturally bright.

It was unsettling. Unearthly. The halls he walked every day now seemed deeply unfamiliar. And having Shouko here with him, three steps ahead, only reinforced this impression.

Half of him was convinced he was dreaming.

He found it hard to believe Shouko was real.

But the other half knew this was actually happening.

His feelings weren't keeping up. His emotions were lagging behind his consciousness. Three steps behind. Same as the distance between the two of them.

He could catch up if he tried. Shouko wasn't walking fast. Closing the gap would be easy.

But Sakuta didn't. He couldn't.

"……"

He was scared that, if he took his eyes off her, she'd vanish.

And so he simply kept pace with her, eyes locked on her back.

Their footsteps echoed. Sakuta didn't know where they were headed. He just trailed after her, like a child following the piper in the fairy tale.

This didn't last long.

Sakuta stopped in his tracks. Consciously, but not by choice.

Shouko had stopped, so he did, too.

"Sakuta," she said, turning to face him. She seemed displeased.

"What?"

"Why are you so far behind?"

"You told me to follow you."

She let out a long sigh.

"Normally, I'd take that as one of your jokes, but you actually mean it?"

Her eyes had a soft reproach. A look that said, "Get a grip, Sakuta."

"It still feels like I'm dreaming," he mumbled. A weak excuse.

"……"

"Are you really here, Shouko?"

It wasn't that he doubted his eyes. And it wasn't that he didn't believe what she had said. That just wasn't enough to banish his fears. He couldn't shake the impression that she'd vanish in the blink of an eye. And that left him deeply anxious. He knew all too well how the things that really mattered could slip from his grasp...and that left him terrified by the prospect of further loss.

"Do I not seem real?"

"...I'm not sure you do."

"Got it."

What she got, he didn't know.

"Go ahead," Shouko said, spreading her arms. "Make sure I'm here."

"……"

Wordlessly, he took a step toward her, then another. And put his arms around her, like it was the most natural thing in the world.

"!"

Shouko radiated voiceless surprise. Sakuta was in no condition to respond. He could feel her pressing up against him. His arms were wrapped around her slender frame. She seemed so fragile. But she was no mirage and wouldn't vanish at his touch. He could feel her weight. She was solid and tangible. Now that he had his arms around her, he didn't ever want to let go.

"You shouldn't take jokes seriously," she croaked.

"I have no sense of humor today."

He was becoming aware of her warmth. The softness of her skin. The regular throb of her pulse...of the life Mai had given her.

"That is so not like you, Sakuta."

"It's still me, though."

"That's concerning."

"……"

"Sakuta, what are we doing next?" she asked in a no-nonsense voice.

"Saving Mai…?"

"Wrong," she said, before he could even finish.

"Wrong how?" he asked, reflexively tightening his arms.

"Okay, Sakuta, if you squeeze any harder, it'll officially count as cheating!"

She hit the exact tone you use to scold a small child, and Sakuta finally let go. He took a step back.

"Wrong how?" he asked again.

He was vaguely aware that he sounded petulant. Again, much like a small child.

He'd said the only thing that mattered. They were saving Mai. Sakuta had followed Shouko here for that purpose, to accomplish that one thing.

"It's all wrong. Every bit of it."

"Then what are we doing?"

He was getting a bit heated. Maybe his deadened emotions were coming back to life. Sakuta was faintly surprised to discover he still had that much left in him. But he couldn't dwell on that now.

"Sakuta…"

"……"

"You're going to meet the one you love."

"……!"

"You're going to make the one you love happy."

"……"

He couldn't speak. The surprise soon faded. All that remained was understanding, seeping into him like water into a sponge.

"And if you've got no sense of humor, can you make Mai happy?"

"……"

Shouko's words got right to the heart of the matter, and that was why he couldn't respond.

That was what saving Mai really meant. What he really wanted to do. It didn't end with saving her life. His goals lay much, much further off. And Shouko had put that in words even a child could understand.

So he couldn't waste time panicking. Or being scared. He had to be calm and collected. To be ready for anything.

That was easier said than done. If anything, it was the opposite of easy. But he couldn't say it was impossible. Saying "I can't" was not an option. That was because he knew a girl who'd pulled it off and done so with a smile.

And she was standing right in front of him.

Shouko was living proof that no matter how hard the road ahead, you could pull through. The warmth of her smile had saved him time and time again. It was doing so right now.

And this knowledge meant he couldn't claim that it couldn't be done. Wouldn't.

"You're amazing, Shouko," he said as he tried to muster a smile to match. He was still having trouble with that. The past few days had left his cheeks as stiff as concrete.

Shouko looked amused. "You pass," she said. "Barely."

"Grading on a curve."

"I've always been soft on you. Is that news?"

"No, I was well aware. Since the moment we first met."

Shouko's smile was a little wobbly. The Shouko he spoke of was a different Shouko, one from a different future. Her reaction drove home the fact that the future had actually changed. A painful reminder that the future ahead of them was one in which Mai did not exist. But that pain was highly motivating.

"So where am I following you to?"

"We're already here."

Shouko looked up at the sign above them. It read NURSE'S OFFICE.

Naturally, the office was empty.

The fluorescent lights were off. They had to rely on the lights of the cars on Route 134, streetlights, house lights, and the faint glow of the moon above.

"Why here?" he asked.

Shouko was doing a circuit of the office, exploring. At one point, she peered into a glass cabinet filled with medical supplies.

"What we're doing requires a bed."

"……"

"Ah! Did your mind go straight to the gutter?"

Grinning impishly, she moved over to the bed.

"Not really in the mood…," Sakuta said.

"That's no fun!" Shouko said, clearly not meaning it. She sat down on the bed. She put the drinks she'd bought at the store on the bedside table. Then she took out some paper cups and poured two drinks.

Sakuta was still standing motionless in the middle of the room, so she beckoned to him, patting the bed beside her. It was an obvious invitation to take a seat.

"The bed isn't the time machine, is it?" he asked, sitting down next to her.

"Now *that* sounds more like the real you," she said with a laugh. "No. Sadly, there is no time machine."

She handed him a paper cup. He'd been running around and crying a lot, so he was pretty thirsty. He accepted the drink and downed it all at once. He tasted plum—accompanied by a burning sensation.

"?! Shouko, this is…"

"A grown-up plum soda," Shouko said with a grin. She hid the empty can in the plastic bag. He didn't see the need to press the point. He'd already polished it off, and—given the circumstances—it was hardly anything more than a harmless prank. Sakuta had much bigger things to think about. There was so much he needed to ask. He was finally settling down. They should probably get to the heart of the matter.

"So how do I get to the past?"

If he was going to accomplish anything, they'd first have to clear that problem. He couldn't save Mai or make her happy without first going back in time.

"The past is always right beside us."

"……"

"Over there, and over there," Shouko said, pointing. Not at anything in particular. But Rio had told him something very similar before, so he didn't question it.

"But you can't usually see it or reach out and touch it," she added.

"I can see and touch you, Shouko."

She let that pass without comment. "Normally, it's all we can do to perceive the present. We don't realize the past and future are all around us."

"……"

"And it's hard to see what you don't know is there."

But Shouko was doing just that. Had done so many times before.

"But you already know, Sakuta. You know the past and present are never far, and that I've come from the future."

He did. He knew all of that. But simply knowing that wouldn't enable time travel. Otherwise, anyone who knew the truth could do it.

"All of this is specific to you, right?" he said. "Adolescence Syndrome makes it possible."

That was the basis for all of this.

Shouko had rejected the future, and her Adolescence Syndrome had, ironically, allowed her to reach this future. Her desire to never grow up had slowed down the world she perceived. But in terms of relativity, time moves slower the faster you go—and as a result, the Shouko who didn't want to grow up had grown up faster than the Shouko who did.

"True. I think that's accurate. But even so—it doesn't explain why I'm here."

"It doesn't?"

"Little me developed Adolescence Syndrome because of her fears about the future. She was physically unable to grow up without a heart transplant, after all."

Her eyes were locked on him, telling him something.

"So…is the present Shouko— Has Makinohara already had her surgery?" he asked.

If that was true, then she was right. It didn't make sense for future Shouko to be here at this point in time.

"Yes, she has."

Her eyes confirmed it. She spoke slowly, as if trying to get through to him.

"After the surgery, I woke up...on the morning of December twenty-seventh."

"......"

He didn't need to look at the clock. It was already the next day. December 28. And it was after sunset. Little Shouko's fears of the future should have been resolved with the success of her transplant. The underlying cause of her Adolescence Syndrome should have been eliminated.

"Then why are you here?"

If little Shouko no longer had Adolescence Syndrome, then logic dictated that big Shouko shouldn't be around anymore. Yet she clearly was.

"I believe what you and I perceive as 'the present' is actually 'the future.'"

"......"

It took him a long time to grasp her meaning.

"Right now, you and I are in the future," Shouko said. "We might be standing here talking, but this is *not* actually the present."

"That can't be..."

"And the one doing this...is you, Sakuta."

Unable to process this, he just gaped at her.

"...Shouko, what...?"

This had to be some sort of sick joke. But Shouko looked totally serious. No signs of her usual teasing. She was holding his gaze, speaking patiently.

"Doesn't ring a bell?"

"...How could...?"

He trailed off. Denying this should be easy. But it wasn't. Maybe part of him already knew.

"Like the little me did, part of you is rejecting the future."

There was only one thing that could make him do that. And Shouko was gently leading him there.

The light of the answer glowed up ahead.

Far ahead.

In the depths of his heart.

He squinted at it, and it began to take shape.

She was right.

He had rejected the future.

With all his might.

He knew exactly when.

The instant he'd learned it was his heart in big Shouko.

And when Mai found out...

——*"Choose a future with me."*

When she'd said that...

——*"Stay with me."*

When she'd broken down crying in the station.

——*"I want to live."*

When he was talking to big Shouko and let the wave of emotions get the best of him.

Sakuta had hoped that December 24, the day of destiny, would never arrive. He knew he had to find an answer, but the whole time he'd been battling his own reluctance to do so. He'd tried to face the part of him that didn't want to make a choice, and he thought he had...but clearly hadn't.

And if that had led him to manifest the same Adolescence Syndrome symptoms as Shouko...

"......"

"Figured it out?"

"......"

He said nothing. His last shred of reason rejected the idea of exposing himself like that.

"I get not wanting to admit it, but we're gonna need you to. You've got to face the weakness inside, the part of you that rejected what the future held."

"Shouko."

"Believing in that weakness is the first step toward admitting you're in the future. And if this is the future, then you can go back to the present. Go back and save Mai."

"……"

He took a deep breath.

He looked down at the empty cup.

Admitting his own weakness.

Running those words through his mind made him laugh—well, it was more a wheeze.

"Sakuta?"

"That part's easy."

He wasn't putting a brave face on it, lying, or joking. He genuinely meant it. He'd found that within himself. Imagined himself clinging to the bottom of the cup.

"No way I could be fine with any of this. It makes far more sense to assume it drove me around the bend."

That idea was much more convincing. He'd thought he was handling stuff better than he'd expected, so being told he really *hadn't* was kind of a relief.

"That side of you is really something, Sakuta."

"You're one to talk, Shouko," he said with a chuckle. "But how exactly do I get to the present?"

"Common sense dictates that whatever you see must be the present. As long as you're trapped by that idea, you can't travel to other times, no matter how close they may be."

"So…abandon all logic, then?"

"You need to discard any logic or rationale that tries to constrain your perception of 'here and now.'"

"Now you sound like Futaba."

"Well, yeah, I got all of this from her."

Shouko puffed up her chest in pride.

"Future Futaba came up with this hypothesis."

"So even in the future, she's providing consultations on Adolescence Syndrome?"

That was a hilarious thought. He loved it.

"Okay, so how do I discard logic?"

He figured common sense would cling to you whether you gave it any conscious thought or not. It wasn't like you could flip a switch in your mind to rid yourself of it. Believing that the past and future were constantly within reach went against all common sense and seemed inherently impossible.

"I told you that already."

Clearly, she wanted him to think for himself. She must have been referring to when they first reached the nurse's office. They hadn't really talked much before getting here.

What was it that she'd said? He tried to remember.

"......"

His brain was still sluggish, but the first thing that came to mind sounded like a joke.

"You mean...go to sleep?"

"Exactly! Best way to abandon common sense is in a dream."

"Hence the nurse's office."

He looked at the bed beneath him. This was definitely the only place in school with one of these.

"But...Shouko..."

"No buts!"

She waggled an index finger at him.

Sakuta shook his head, pressing on.

"Even if I can go back in time..."

If he saved Mai, that mostly likely meant Shouko wouldn't have a future. The fact that Mai had been able to replace Sakuta as a donor was already astronomically unlikely. A future in which he saved Mai from the accident and survived it himself...how would Shouko fare in that scenario?

He meant to say all of this out loud but couldn't. Shouko didn't let him. She reached out and pinched his cheek.

"No buts."

"……"

"You can't wimp out on me now!"

She was scolding him again. Lips pursed. But his eyes were on something else: her left hand, pinching his cheek. The sparkle on her finger. A simple silver ring. All his attention had snapped right to it.

"Oh…," Shouko said, noticing his gaze. She quickly withdrew her hand and put her other hand over it, almost hiding it. Her fingers touched the ring. She spun it in place, as if reminding herself how it felt.

Big Shouko had appeared many times before but never with a ring. But the Shouko from the future where he survived? She had one. The meaning of that wasn't lost on him. And of course, if he changed things now, that future would also change. Just like this Shouko had Mai's heart instead of his.

"Your ring…"

"Always wanted to get married in college."

She grinned, like she was trying to cover an awkward moment. And that smile betrayed the happiness of her life, like the warmth of the spring sun. But behind it, he found a note of sadness.

"What I want, Sakuta," she said, gazing through the window at the ocean, "is for the one I love to be happy. I want him to smile. Even if it isn't for me."

"…Shouko."

At her name, she turned and grinned at him again.

"I'm very persistent."

"……"

"Until you're happy, I'll keep coming back from any future to help you. No matter how many times it takes."

There was determination hidden behind that impish grin. It wasn't overbearing, but there was an undeniable strength to it. One that shone through her words and bearing.

"So stop resisting and be happy."

What a merciless phrase. But at the same time—it was very Shouko.

"……"

"……"

There was a brief silence, punctuated with the sound of passing cars on Route 134. He never noticed that sound when school was in session, but with no other noises, it sure was tugging at his attention.

"Shouko," he said, making up his mind.

"What, Sakuta?"

She'd given him the space he needed. So he didn't hesitate to say the rest.

"I'll make Mai happy."

It came out easily.

"Yes, I'm sure you will."

"……"

"Only you can."

"So there's something I need to say to you."

"……"

Here, Shouko shook her head. Her eyes said there was no need. But Sakuta wasn't about to be dissuaded.

Shouko had made him realize something.

And he'd made his decision in light of that.

And he owed it to Shouko to explain his decision.

Going back in time would only get him just that—time. Maybe he'd find a way to keep Mai from getting hit by that van, but if he did, then Shouko would lose her donor.

And if he was going to make Mai happy, then Sakuta couldn't get hit by a van, either. Losing Mai had made him all too aware of how much grief his own death would put her through.

And he couldn't do that to her.

So he had to say it.

"I want you to live, Shouko."

His calm voice filled the nurse's office.

"From the bottom of my heart, I hope Makinohara gets the transplant she needs."

"Okay."

"I'm praying for you."

A little bit at time.

"I'm wishing on every star."

He told her how he truly felt.

"I know," she said.

"But I'm not a doctor."

"......"

"And I don't have any special abilities or powers."

"......"

"I'm just a high school kid."

"You've got a lot more nerve than most of them."

A little laugh escaped him. This made it a little easier for both of them, he thought. But when he was done, he kept going. Putting all his feelings in words.

"It's all I can do to make Mai happy."

"......"

"And I couldn't even do that right."

He broke off, emotions choking his voice. He felt tears welling up, but it didn't seem right to cry in front of Shouko. So he fought them back. He looked up, waiting for the heat behind his nose to go away. He stayed like that for a good ten seconds.

"So," he said. "That means one thing, Shouko."

"Yes."

"I can't do anything for you."

He looked her right in the eye as he said it.

This was the path he'd chosen.

Maybe some would say it was a selfish choice.

Maybe some would accuse him of making a mistake.

Maybe some would curse his lack of morals.

But Sakuta was fine with all of that.

Selfish, mistaken, or immoral—fine.

If he could make Mai happy, it was worth it.

"Sakuta, that's how it should be."

She was wearing her usual smile. There was just one difference—that flawless smile of hers was wet with tears.

"...Shouko?"

"Mm...?"

She'd only just noticed.

"Why...am I...?"

She wiped the tears with her fingers.

"I swore I wouldn't..."

"......"

"I guess hearing it out loud...still hit me pretty hard."

Shouko offered an excuse in apparent consternation about her tears. She kept insisting that she was fine, like she was worried about how he'd take it. She never once looked sad. Just a little embarrassed by her crying.

She was trying to act tough for his sake, and he wanted to say something, to tell her how that made him feel.

"......"

He opened his mouth to do just that but ultimately said nothing more.

There was nothing else he could do for her.

He'd already said everything he had to say. So he swallowed apologies and gratitude alike and just watched, waiting for Shouko to recover.

The tears on her fingers glistened in the moonlight.

The silver ring gleamed on her left ring finger.

"One last thing," Sakuta said, despite himself.

"Yes?"

"When you get back to the future, deliver a message to future me."

"......"

"Tell him, 'Make your adorable bride the happiest person in the world.'"

"......!"

For a moment, Shouko was caught off guard. That told him everything. He'd figured as much, but now he was sure. He wasn't talking to Shouko Makinohara. He was talking to Shouko Azusagawa.

"......I'll make sure he hears that," Shouko said, smiling softly through her tears. They were dripping off her cheeks, and she was no longer trying to wipe them away. This time they were tears of joy.

Shouko stood up.

"Time you lay down, Sakuta."

To go back in time, he had to abandon common sense. And that could only be done in dreams. She had just explained this to him.

"Ever since it happened...I've never been quite sure if I was awake or not."

He wasn't sure he'd actually fall asleep.

"I'm worried that..."

But a yawn interrupted him.

His eyelids felt heavy.

"You'll be fine," Shouko said.

He looked up at her.

"How can you...?"

Shouko was getting blurry. Sakuta felt like he'd slurred his words. This wasn't normal.

"There's nothing to worry about."

Her voice sounded far away. She was right next to him, but it didn't seem like it.

"Shouko...?"

"I made sure to dose your drink."

There was a package of sleeping pills in her hand.

"Oh...okay...that explains it..."

His eyes closed and the world went dark.

"Good night, Sakuta."

Feeling like this had happened to him before, Sakuta sensed his mind drifting off to the world of dreams.

"First, look for someone who can find you."

Pondering the meaning of Shouko's last words, Sakuta embarked on a journey through time.

Chapter

2

Before the snow stops

1

A chill wind on his cheeks.

A winter breeze, carrying the faint scent of the sea.

That cold air pulled Sakuta's mind back to consciousness.

"……"

His eyes snapped open.

The first thing he saw was a white ceiling. A patterned white, with gray marks scattered here and there. He recognized it as the ceiling at school, but he'd never looked up at it lying flat on his back before, so the experience felt novel.

He was lying on the bed in the nurse's office.

He sat up slowly. The bed creaked beneath him, like the cry of some wild thing.

Beckoned by the flow of cold air, Sakuta parted the curtains and peered out.

"……"

The sight that greeted him made him stop dead in his tracks.

There was snow outside the windows. From the school, he could see snow falling over the waters of Shichirigahama. Falling softly but quite heavily.

The sky was blanketed in heavy clouds, with no sign of the sun.

Sakuta's eyes wandered, searching—until he spotted a shelf by the bed. There was a digital clock on it.

The display showed 1:25 PM.

And the date: December 24.

"I'm…really back?"

He hadn't doubted it. It wasn't that he hadn't believed. Naturally, this was what he'd wanted from the bottom of his heart.

But now that it was actually happening, he couldn't help feeling astonished. At the same time, underneath the shock of this moment was a growing conviction. He felt like the cold air on his skin was the cause.

He remembered this chill.

The memory had settled into his very bones.

The freezing, snow-laden winter air.

The air he'd felt on *that* day. This day, December 24.

The whiteness of the snow made his chest ache. The sight of Mai's blood staining that snow was still burned into his eyelids.

Mentally, he knew that was in the future, but a wave of panic was rising up from the soles of his feet. Winding around his body, leaving him barely able to breathe. It felt like he was lifting off the ground.

He was glad to be back before the accident.

But that brought stress with it—this time, he really *couldn't* fail. He *had* to keep Mai from getting hit by that sliding van. And that *need* was rooting him to the spot.

He looked at the clock again.

1:28 PM.

"I was right about the time, then."

Sakuta had been sure he'd return to this very moment. This was when he'd been at the hospital. Shouko's hospital.

And her mother had arranged for him to see little Shouko in the ICU. He remembered staring at her through the glass. A clean room, filled with the hum of machinery. A bed surrounded by medical apparatuses. A young Shouko sleeping on it, desperately clinging to life.

He'd only been there five minutes.

He didn't really remember leaving. The next real memory he had was that evening.

He'd just been sitting still in a chair at the hospital, unable to decide what to do. He wanted a future with Mai and wanted Shouko to have a future, too, but there was no way to have both, so he'd simply stopped thinking at all.

If he'd manifested Adolescence Syndrome at some point, it was definitely then. Nothing else made any sense. And all that led to Sakuta coming back from the future.

"It sure is piling up…"

A voice echoed through the office. Not Sakuta's. A woman's voice, from somewhere nearby.

The nurse was standing by an open window. A woman in her late thirties, wearing a white coat. She was only three yards from him.

"Gonna have to leave my car," she said and closed the window.

Then her eyes turned toward him.

"……"

Sakuta stiffened instinctively. He had no idea how long he'd been sleeping here. Or what her perception of events was. If he'd just appeared on the bed without her knowledge, she might freak out. He'd need a good explanation. He couldn't very well tell her he'd come from the future. She'd never believe that. He'd be worried if she did.

Best to wait and see how she responded. If he had to bullshit an explanation, it was better to follow her lead.

But his plans came up empty.

"……"

The nurse didn't say a word.

Sakuta was only a few yards away, but she didn't even seem to notice him.

"……?"

It didn't seem *that* strange at first. But as she moved around making sure each of the windows was locked, she got much closer, and his concerns mounted.

She stood right next to him, reaching up for the window lock. She essentially had to brush against Sakuta to get to it. And then she walked straight past him a second time, back to her desk and the space heater.

This was clearly weird. Her total lack of reaction wasn't normal.

"Nurse?" he said, abandoning silence.

"……"

She didn't seem to hear him at all. She was writing something in the office journal.

"Nurse!" He tried again, louder. It was basically a yell. It echoed through the room.

"……"

But she still didn't turn and look at him.

It didn't seem like she was ignoring him. Every indication said she genuinely couldn't hear him.

He moved closer and put his hand on her shoulder, calling again.

She still didn't see him. Didn't turn toward him or respond at all. Didn't seem to feel the weight of his hand on her shoulder.

"What in the…?"

This wave of surprise came from his own sensations. His hand was resting on the nurse's shoulder, but he couldn't feel her. Not the texture of her white coat, not the heat of her body, not the soft yield of her skin beneath.

"What's going on?"

He tried to leave the office to find out.

And just as he did, the door opened.

"Nurse, he jammed a finger."

It was Sakuta's friend Yuuma Kunimi. He was wearing shorts and a T-shirt despite the snow. It must have been for basketball practice. He was with a younger boy who was clutching his finger.

"Kunimi!" Sakuta cried.

"Let's get a compress on that," the nurse said. "Sit."

Yuuma didn't react, either. Nobody did.

It wasn't just the nurse who couldn't see Sakuta.

Neither Yuuma nor his teammate could hear Sakuta's voice.

Nobody could see him.

Nobody could hear him.

Nobody noticed his touch.

Sakuta was in real trouble here.

Why was this happening to him?

Looking for answers, his eyes turned to the window.

"......?"

That was when he discovered that something else was wrong.

"......"

Each time Yuuma or the nurse moved, their reflections did, too. But not Sakuta.

Sakuta didn't have a reflection at all.

He reached up and touched himself. He could see himself. See and touch. He could feel his own body.

But nobody else here had noticed him. If they had, at least one of them would've said, "What are you *doing*?" He was acting weird enough to warrant it.

Faced with this predicament, two thoughts came to mind.

First, just before he came back...

The words Shouko had said as he drifted off.

——"*First, look for someone who can find you.*"

He'd had no idea what she meant by that or why she'd said it.

But now he could safely assume she'd been referring to this.

Secondly, the memorable events of last spring.

May, the last day of Golden Week, the day he'd met a wild bunny girl.

The incident that brought him and Mai together—and one caused by Mai's Adolescence Syndrome.

She'd been wearing a bunny-girl costume because nobody else could perceive her—exactly like Sakuta now.

Rio had helped him out then. How had she explained it?

He tugged at the thread of his memories.

The first thing he remembered was the half-dead, half-living cat in a box. Schrödinger's cat.

He remembered a weird thing about the cat's survival only being determined when you opened the box to check.

Apparently, on a quantum, micro level, particles existed probabilistically, and their exact positions in space weren't set—and the only way to determine their locations was to observe them.

That seemed to perfectly describe Sakuta's current state. Half in the future and half in the present—existing only in terms of probability.

Until somebody detected him, he wouldn't actually exist in this timeline. That seemed the most likely application of the concept anyway.

He felt like he had a handle on things now.

But who exactly would be able to detect him? It certainly wasn't the nurse or even his friend here. Neither of them could see him.

"Yo, Kunimi!" he tried again, just to be sure.

"I'm gonna head back." Yuuma clearly had no idea Sakuta was there. He didn't so much as glance his way. it wasn't like he was consciously choosing to ignore him, either.

Grabbing Yuuma by the shoulders and shaking him didn't help. Nothing Sakuta did got through. And nothing Yuuma did affected Sakuta.

Yuuma just left the room like nothing had happened.

No point staying here. Sakuta followed his friend out into the hall. Yuuma headed toward the gym, but Sakuta went the other way. Down the dark, quiet halls—classes were done for the day. Nobody turned to yell, "No running in the halls!"

It was only a hundred-odd-yard dash. Probably only took a dozen or so seconds.

He pulled to a stop outside the science lab.

"Futaba!" he yelled, sliding the door open.

He'd hoped to get a look of scorn. For Rio to turn and glower at him briefly, only to immediately go back to her experiment. Then sigh and say, "More trouble?"

But none of those wishes came true.

"……"

The only sound in the science lab was water bubbling in a beaker.

With this snow, there was no one in the yard. No shouts from the baseball or soccer teams.

But the lights in the room were on, so Sakuta stepped in and closed the door behind him. He felt like it grew even quieter.

He heard something in the silence. One other sound, somewhere in the room.

He stepped up to the experiment table by the chalkboard and put the lid on the alcohol lamp, snuffing out the flame. The boiling water died down, leaving only the sound of someone slowly breathing.

Rio was sound asleep on the table. Using her arms as a pillow, her head leaning gently to one side. He could only make out half her face.

She looked tired. There were tear tracks on her cheeks. He knew exactly why. The answer was on the board in front of him—behind Rio.

A complicated formula and a mystery graph. The names Azusagawa and Shouko and the words *present* and *future*.

She'd clearly been erasing and redoing it over and over. There was a ton of half-erased marks on the board, and it was a far lighter shade than its usual dark green. And there was a huge X through the working theory she had up there now.

Scattered on the table around her were books from the school and public libraries.

"……"

It took his breath away.

This wasn't for one of Rio's club experiments.

She'd been searching for a way out.

Trying to find a way to save both Sakuta and Shouko.

She must have been working on this ever since she learned it was Sakuta's heart inside big Shouko. She'd likely gone days without much sleep as she worked on the problem.

Sakuta had been too focused on his own mess to even notice how hard Rio was working. She was suffering, too, struggling against fate along with him. Refusing to give up until she was too tired to wait for her coffee.

And she hadn't found the answer she wanted.

"Thank you, Futaba."

He moved around behind her and found her coat by her bag. He draped it over her shoulders.

"......"

She didn't wake up. If that had been enough to wake her and make her notice him, she'd have done so when he came in.

When he placed his hand on Rio's shoulder, he felt nothing. While he was touching her, all sensations vanished from his body. Not just touch, but his sense of his body's size, heat, and weight—all gone.

"Can't even have any fun being an invisible man."

He wasn't talking to anyone in particular. It was just him griping about the whole dang thing. The passing comment was couched in the hope that saying something would stave off the rising sense of panic.

Sakuta had to think of a way to make someone perceive him. And since he couldn't ask Rio for help, he'd have to do that on his own.

His eyes lit on Rio's bag. And the phone in the pocket on it.

"Gonna borrow this a sec," he said out of habit.

He started to dial a number, but his finger was suddenly shaking. These eleven digits were Mai's cell phone number. If he hit the call button, he might hear her voice. The anticipation got the better of him, sending tremors from his head to his toes.

He managed to hit the button and put the phone to his ear.

"......?"

It didn't take long to realize something was wrong.

He couldn't hear anything.

He checked the screen. The device was showing a call in progress. But when he held it to his ear, there was nothing ringing, no voice on the other end. No faint static of a call picked up.

He dialed again.

"......"

Same results.

He tried a different number. The number of the apartment he and his sister, Kaede, lived in. A landline.

Big Shouko was staying with them. She should have been there. She was from the future, so he hoped she could see and hear him. He had a lot of hopes riding on this call.

But just like Mai's number, it didn't even ring. The call wouldn't connect. No matter how many times he tried, the outcome stayed the same.

"Okay, so phones aren't an option."

He opened Futaba's contact list, searching for Mai's entry. He knew Mai and Rio e-mailed each other sometimes, and he found her address listed as "Sakurajima-senpai." He typed, "This is Sakuta," and hit send.

"......"

There was no response. The phone didn't budge at all.

Logic failed him here, but it was clear his voice and words weren't getting through to anybody. He was forced to accept this as fact even if he didn't understand why.

Maybe he really was the cat in the box.

The lid was firmly closed and locked. Slamming against the walls accomplished nothing. No vibrations or sounds reached the world outside.

He had no way to tell anyone he existed. All he could do was wait for someone to open the box.

He felt like Mai would have a key. There was no real basis for him to believe that, of course. Just faith that she'd be able to detect his presence.

But Mai wasn't here. On December 24, she was at a studio in the city, filming interior scenes for her movie. And Sakuta had no idea where that studio was.

If phones and e-mail were out of the picture, he had no way of asking her himself.

"So I'm in deep shit, huh?"

Sakuta figured this was a calm and accurate assessment of his predicament.

The only time and place he was sure he could meet up with Mai was right before the accident. He knew for a fact that she'd be there in front of the Benten Bridge at six. To save this timeline's Sakuta…

"…But that's not an option."

It was too uncertain. Even if he managed to find Mai in the Christmas crowds, what if she couldn't see him? He couldn't leave things to the last minute.

And worse, if he stepped in to save her then, there'd be nothing to stop this timeline's Sakuta—present Sakuta.

According to what Rio had told him before, the way quantum stuff worked meant future Sakuta and present Sakuta would never meet.

In other words, he—future Sakuta—couldn't be the one to stop his past self—present Sakuta. He couldn't run up to himself, punch himself in the face, and stop himself from going to the scene of the accident. He had to assume that wasn't an option.

His best shot was to find a way to tell present Sakuta and Mai what was going to happen before it did.

But to do that, he needed someone to open the box, to perceive Sakuta's presence in this timeline.

The question was—who?

Who else might have a key? Shouko? Future Shouko, who'd received his heart in a transplant. Emotionally, it made sense that if he'd been able to perceive her, she'd be able to perceive him.

He had an idea where she might be. He knew she'd spent the morning of the twenty-fourth in Sakuta's apartment. She'd seen him off at the door on his way to school. He remembered her smile.

"It's my best bet."

Part of him thought relying on her *again* was pretty sad, especially since what he was trying to do would nip her future in the bud. He shouldn't be forcing her to help with that. A few days ago, that thought would have been enough to give him pause. But not anymore. His mind was made up.

"……"

It didn't make it hurt any less. But he'd chosen this path. He'd chosen to build a future with Mai. And he'd do whatever it took to achieve that, no matter what.

Sakuta put Rio's phone back in her bag and turned to leave the science lab. He fully intended to head straight home in hopes of finding big Shouko.

But as he opened the door, he paused. He'd heard movement behind him.

He swung back around.

"Was I…?" Rio muttered, sitting up. Still half-asleep. The coat he'd put on her shoulders fell to the floor.

"……"

Rio stared at the coat, puzzled. Then she picked it up, dusted it off, and placed it on top of her bag.

She glanced around the lab table. There was still steam rising from the beaker on the wire net. But the lid was on the alcohol lamp below it. Rio held a hand over that, feeling the heat.

"…Still warm," she murmured.

She looked around the room with a frown.

"Futaba?" Sakuta called, moving closer. Maybe she'd noticed him. She was getting his hopes up. "I'm right here!" he yelled.

"The teacher must have stopped by…," Rio concluded.

"No, it was me!" he protested with a note of desperation in his voice.

But her eyes never focused on him. He was right across the table, but Rio couldn't see him. She looked right through him at the ceiling beyond. If she could see him at all, her eyes would never focus there.

"Earth to Futaba! I'm right in front of you!"

He waved a hand in front of her face. Even cupped her cheeks at one point. No use.

Rio just turned her back on him, her attention on the chalkboard once more.

She picked up the chalk and began writing something.

Sakuta moved around the table and wrote *Look at me, Futaba!* in big letters.

Rio didn't turn around.

She couldn't see what he'd written. She scribbled her formula right over his letters, heedless of how unreadable the results were.

"Guess I really *can't* rely on you this time, huh?"

Given his predicament, there was no one he wanted to talk to more. Having that option off the table was terrifying. She'd always helped him before…

But at the same time, he still remembered everything she'd told him so far.

Rio had taught him about the potentially dead cat, and that was helping him deal with being imperceptible.

Understanding the underlying principles did a lot to ease the confusion of a truly bizarre situation.

It gave him direction, an idea what he needed to do and accomplish.

He had to find someone who could detect him.

And it was Rio's words that gave him a hint who that might be.

"Maybe I should have paid a *little* more attention…"

Too late to regret that now.

Putting it out of his mind, he headed toward the hall again. He needed to get home right away.

But on his way to the exit, he stopped in his tracks.

Outside the faculty office…

…something caught his eye.

A rack of costumes used for the culture or sports festivals. They must have just been delivered by the cleaners. Each was in a plastic bag with a numbered tag.

And one of them was a bunny costume.

Sakuta remembered the day he met Mai.

The wild bunny girl in the Shonandai Library.

"Let's take a cue from Mai here."

Sakuta reached for the bunny costume.

2

"This is actually not bad."

Sakuta had come back from the future in a school tracksuit, so the bunny outfit was providing a lot of protection against the snow and cold.

He'd left his shoes in the future, too. The costume also helped with that.

It came with a full headpiece, but he needed to see, so he carried that under his arm.

He first headed to Shichirigahama Station.

He didn't have his train pass or the money to buy a ticket, but since nobody could see him anyway, he just walked right in and boarded a train bound for Fujisawa.

He grabbed a spot by the door and scoped out the car.

It was packed with passengers traveling in from the Kamakura area, but nobody seemed to notice him or his costume. If anyone had, no doubt he'd be hearing a lot of whispers.

"Isn't that crazy?"

"He crazy."

"So crazy."

And lots of stifled smirks. But nobody did anything like that. Not one person met his eye and hastily looked away.

It was like he was made of air.

Last spring, when Mai had been grappling with her Adolescence Syndrome, this must have been what she'd felt like.

It was very different from typical ostracization.

If people were ignoring you, you felt ignored—but Sakuta wasn't even getting that.

He just…felt nothing.

This gave him a newfound understanding of why Mai had chosen to walk around in a racy bunny-girl outfit. That was just how badly she'd wanted someone to see her.

The outfits might make them look ridiculous, but being imperceptible was just that terrifying—for Sakuta now, and Mai back then. He was ready to clutch at any straw.

"I've still got her bunny-girl outfit."

When this was all over, he'd have to ask her to wear it again.

He glanced out the windows as the train pulled into Enoshima Station. Half the passengers got out, but just as many got on.

None of the new arrivals could see Sakuta, either. He was standing by the door, right in their line of sight, but nobody even glanced his way.

Without anyone noticing him, he reached Fujisawa Station—the end of the line.

He hopped off first, moved to the exit gates, and turned back to scan the platform. Then he flung out both costumed arms.

"Can anybody see me?!" he yelled, loud enough to fill the station.

He felt very silly, but a hundred people filed past him, running their cards through the gates—none of them aware of his antics.

Nobody here saw Sakuta. Nobody noticed that their shoulders bumped his. Sakuta couldn't feel the impact, so he was certain they didn't, either.

Not letting this get him down, he turned and left the station.

As he passed through the JR station, he stowed the costume's head in a locker. It was a good ten-minute walk from here to his apartment—maybe five if he ran. The big head would only slow him down.

He used the same locker Mai had kept her bunny-girl outfit in. It just happened to be empty, so he went with it.

He didn't have a coin to lock it.

"It'll be fine."

Right now, Sakuta had an impenetrable invisibility barrier. Worrying about a costume head seemed like a complete waste of time.

With his arms free, he ran out into the snow. The cold air tore at his lungs and made his nose hurt.

Five minutes later, badly out of breath, he was outside the apartment building where he and Kaede lived. Kaede had left the day before to stay with their grandparents, so if anyone was here, it would be big Shouko—and of course, their calico cat, Nasuno.

Sakuta stood at the entrance, peering through the auto lock doors. He hadn't brought his key back from the future, so he didn't have a way of getting into his own home.

He tried the intercom.

He punched their apartment number and hit the call button. This was surprisingly difficult. He lived here, so he'd never used it. He always just used his key.

"Is it ringing?"

He wasn't even sure.

Just to be sure, he punched in his room number again and tried once more.

"……"

He waited, but no answer came.

He'd been hoping Shouko would answer.

He wanted to try the apartment door next, but without a key, he'd have to wait here for someone to go in or out.

Figuring pacing back and forth would just wear him out, he sat down and leaned against the wall. He was working against a time limit here, and sitting still wasn't doing his mental health any favors. He could feel the impatience rising up within him.

When he'd caught his breath again, he got to his feet.

Hoping to distract himself, he looked in their mailbox.

And found something unexpected.

"…Huh."

There was a key inside.

It looked familiar.

He was sure it was the key to his apartment. The spare he'd given Shouko while she was staying with them.

It was a challenge picking the key up with the costume on, but he managed it.

It also took a gratingly long time to get it in the keyhole and open the front door.

He took the elevator to the fifth floor.

He ran down the hall to his apartment. The door was locked, so he opened it.

"Shouko!" he called, already certain she wasn't here. He had to know for sure, though.

No answer came.

No one came out to welcome him.

"Shouko!" he called, bursting into the living room.

He was met with the specific quiet of an empty apartment. Only the whirr of the heater at work.

No sign of Shouko in Sakuta's room, in Kaede's room, in the toilet, in the bathroom, or in the closet.

The room was clean and tidy. The kitchen sink was polished and gleaming, not a drop of water anywhere. Even the dishes always left on the drying rack were put away in the cabinets. The *kotatsu* futon had been straightened out. It felt like a showroom for a housing development project, like no one had ever lived here.

Shouko had wiped away every sign of her presence.

The key from the mailbox was the only thing she'd left behind.

She'd promised to meet him at six for a date. By the dragon lanterns in front of Benten Bridge.

And he was just now finding out how early she'd left. He'd had no idea she'd cleaned this thoroughly, erasing herself like this. His head had been too full of Mai to notice the state of the room.

"......"

Back in the living room, he stopped moving—until something hopped up on the *kotatsu*. Their cat, Nasuno. She was why they left the heat on all day.

Nasuno seemed to be staring at him.

"Nasuno?" he said, and she turned away, scratching her neck with a hind leg. Then she hid back under the *kotatsu*.

He'd thought she could see him, but it must have been his imagination.

"...I'm doomed."

Saying it out loud seemed to provoke a physical reaction—a chill ran down his spine.

First he couldn't find Mai, now Shouko.

Kaede was at their grandparents, too far to reach in time. It was two hours either way, and the trip there and back would take until after six. With no guarantee she'd even be able to see him, it wasn't a good risk to take.

"I've just gotta find a crowd, I guess."

Maybe *someone* would see him. This felt like betting on a miracle, but at least it would be more productive than standing in the living room staring at a cat.

Giving up wasn't an option.

That choice did not exist.

He opened the fridge and took out a bottle with a blue label. The sports drink Mai did commercials for. A big two-liter. It was a third full, but he chugged the whole thing.

Rehydrated, he dropped the empty bottle on the counter and was out the front door an instant later.

Sakuta was back at Fujisawa Station.

At the heart of a city of four hundred thousand.

Most of the inhabitants passed through here every day.

Three train lines stopped at this station—JR, Odakyu, and the Enoden. The area was packed no matter what time you arrived.

It was just after two thirty, and there were lots of junior high and high school students in uniform. Plenty of college groups and couples, too. They were all off to Enoshima to enjoy Christmas like the young are wont to do. A lot of them were excited by the faint dusting of snow.

On the opposite end of the spectrum were young business types, lots of suits and ties. These were looking up at the sky with expressions even gloomier than the clouds above. Most opened umbrellas before leaving the station awning.

Sakuta was wandering aimlessly though these crowds.

No umbrella, still dressed as a bunny.

Nobody paid him any attention.

Dusting the snow off his shoulders, he walked into the station. He took the head out of the locker and put it on, but this did not attract any attention.

They were still completely oblivious to his presence. Not even that— he had no presence. They didn't even perceive him in the first place. Sakuta did not exist.

But he called out, hoping against hope that somebody out there would hear him.

"Can anybody see me?!"

He slapped the hands of his costume together as he jumped up and down.

"Come on! Look at me!"

Every few minutes, a train pulled in, carrying another flood of people. Sakuta was facing the JR gates. Another stream was coming up behind him from the Odakyu Enoshima Line and the Enoden.

There seemed to be even more people than usual. Probably the holiday. Lots of people went to Enoshima for Christmas Eve dates.

"Hello!"

Far too many people to count. Hundreds wouldn't cut it. There were thousands passing him by.

But none of them could see Sakuta. Or hear him yelling.

Less than twenty minutes of this, and his voice stopped working. The exhaustion caught up with him, and he just couldn't summon the energy.

At the thirty-minute mark, Sakuta noticed an emotion growing inside him.

Fear, spreading like a vine, its tendrils invading every inch of him, winding around his heart, locking his body in its grip.

He didn't plan on giving up.

But…what if he couldn't do anything?

That possibility was ballooning up inside, tearing away at him.

"Somebody! Anybody!" he yelled, trying to fight the fear. "Can anyone hear my voice?"

He looked left and right, watching the people around him. People running to catch their next train. People stopping to muck with their phones. People calling friends or laughing with whoever they'd been waiting for.

Every type of person—except the type that could see Sakuta.

"Please listen! Hear my voice!"

The kernel of fear grew one size larger.

It suddenly seemed all too possible that he might still be doing this at six.

The fateful accident might happen again.

That thought made him tremble.

He didn't want to remember.

The vehicle knocking over the signpost.

A black minivan.

Mai curled up next to it.

Her body on the snow. Unmoving.

And a pool of her blood turning the white to red.

The ambulance came and couldn't save her.

The hospital they took her to…couldn't save her.

——*"By the time she reached us, it was already too late."*

The doctor's words, post-surgery, still echoed in Sakuta's ears. He tried to peel them away, but they came back up at the slightest provocation, rattling his heart. Squeezing it. Ever since, he'd been bound by invisible chains that prevented him from doing anything.

And that horrible future might happen again.

If Sakuta didn't change it.

And if this *was* the present, this time he couldn't try again.

He couldn't fail. Failure was not an option. There was no next time.

"Hey! Listen up! Hear me!"

His voice got more desperate as Sakuta tried to keep the fear at bay.

"There's gotta be *someone!*"

He wasn't scared that nobody could see him.

"There has to be *one*!"

He wasn't scared of being alone.

"Come on!"

He was scared of losing Mai.

"Hear me!"

Scared of not saving her.

"Can anyone see me?"

He found a man staring at his phone and grabbed his shoulder.

"Can you see me?"

He tugged the arm of a station attendant.

"Please! I just need *one*!"

He clung to a passing police officer.

"Find me!"

But there was no one. So many people were filling the station to the brim—and still nobody could see Sakuta.

"Give me a chance to save Mai…"

He squeezed those words out. A heartfelt plea.

"Please. I'm begging you."

But his pleas and cries went unheard. To them, Sakuta's begging did not exist.

The ebb and flow of the crowd felt featureless and hollow. Every person in that crowd had a face, but they all looked the same to Sakuta. He could no longer tell anyone apart. And once that happened, his vision swam. He felt dizzy. He found himself on the ground. His knees had buckled.

He tried to stand but lacked the strength.

He'd thought he was still hanging in there emotionally, but his body had instinctively given up.

This senseless nightmare had become unbearable.

Sakuta tried again, straining the muscles in his legs.

All he had to show for it was the hiss of air escaping his lungs.

Then a shadow fell over him.

All he could see were the tiles on the ground—and then a pair of feet stopped in front of him. Navy socks, brown shoes—typical high school girl fashion.

"What are you *doing*, senpai?"

A voice called to him from above. He recognized it.

Even if he hadn't, there was only one person who called him "senpai."

"Koga...," he rasped, lifting his head.

Before him stood a petite high school girl wearing a Minegahara uniform with a coat on over it. A cute brown one. She had fluffy short hair and flawless makeup. But the look on her face was the opposite of cute. She was staring down at him with a mix of disgust, confusion, and alarm. But her eyes were clearly focused on him.

"...You can see me?" he asked, his lips and voice shaking.

"What are you talking about?"

She genuinely didn't seem to know. He saw himself reflected in her eyes.

"...You can hear me?"

"I can hear *and* see you. Look, everyone's staring."

Tomoe glanced at the crowd around them, seeming embarrassed.

"Huh?"

The moment she said it, he could feel eyes on him. Countless people were looking. Nobody went so far as to stop moving, but the stream of people going in and out of the gates were all glancing at Sakuta in passing. Seeing a weird kid in a bunny costume sitting on the ground was out of the ordinary.

"Ha..."

That was his honest opinion on the matter. In a single instant, he'd gone from backed into a corner to wide-open horizons. Someone had opened the lid of the box he'd been trapped in. He was suddenly actually here.

And Tomoe had done that for him. She had found him.

"Senpai, have you completely lost it?"

There was an extremely wary look in her eyes.

She really could see him. Really could hear his voice.

As that realization finally seeped in, his hands reached for her legs.

"Holy— Stop that!"

Tomoe quickly backed away.

"Come on, don't run."

"You're the one going for the bad touch!"

"What's so bad about ankles?"

"Last thing I need is snide comments about chubby ankles, too," she muttered.

"Then I'll settle for calves."

"That's worse!"

"I don't care where, but you have to let me touch you."

"……"

Tomoe gaped at him, eyes half-lidded, clearly beyond words.

"You definitely took that the wrong way," Sakuta said.

"I take it that you're a public menace."

"Where can I touch you?"

"I don't want you touching me at all!"

This wasn't getting him anywhere.

"Fine. You touch me instead."

"……"

Tomoe made the exact same face. Like she'd spied some filth on the pavement.

"Save whatever fetish this is for Sakurajima," she grumbled.

"Nah, this isn't…"

He tried to explain himself but couldn't find the words. If he went for the whole story, it would take forever, and even if he did that, she likely wouldn't believe him. And if she *did* believe him, it would just make her worried. This whole thing was inherently concerning.

"Senpai, have you aged years since I last saw you?" she asked, interrupting his reverie.

"Huh?"

"You look like crap," she clarified. She'd knelt down and was peering into his face.

"I can imagine."

"……"

Tomoe seemed taken aback. She must not have expected him to agree with her.

"This is weird."

"How so?"

"You'd normally be all, 'Well, you're fat! Especially your butt!' Like you just love harassing me so much."

"As if. I don't do that."

"You totally do! Like three times a week."

"Wish it was four."

"See? You know you do."

"If it seriously bothers you, just say the word and I'll stop."

"……"

Backing off just seemed to make Tomoe even more disgruntled. She was straight-up scowling now.

"You're *really* weird today."

"I'm always weird."

"True, but…"

She seemed unconvinced.

"Argh! Okay. Fine."

She angrily held out both hands.

"Touch my damn hands, then."

"That was one way to say that."

"Oh, who cares! Just get it over with."

"Don't mind if I do."

He put his fluffy paws on Tomoe's tiny hands and held them tight.

"On-a-counta-three!" he said, going for the Fukuoka-style cheer.

Still holding her hands.

Savoring the feel of her palms.

"Yeesh, leggo a me!"

Tomoe snatched her hands away, turning bright red.

Sakuta had definitely felt her hands. They were tiny but absolutely real. His sense of touch was normal again and he couldn't be happier.

"D-don't make it weird, senpai."

"I'm not."

"You did! I mean, my hands…" She hesitated.

So he said, "Koga, I need you."

"……!"

She got even redder. All the way to her ears. The cold wasn't caus-ing *that*. Their eyes met, and she hastily looked away.

"I-I'm not reading too much into that, I swear," she explained.

He hadn't even said anything yet.

"So what do you need from me?" she asked, with only a hint of spite.

3

He normally walked to the hospital, but today they boarded a bus. It was hard walking through all this snow, and time was of the essence.

Sakuta moved to the back and sat on a seat for two, but instead of sitting down next to him, Tomoe took a seat in front of his. Sakuta's costume was drawing a lot of attention, and she clearly wanted to pre-tend she didn't know him.

"Oh, right, Koga…"

"……"

She even ignored him when he spoke.

"Did you have plans?"

"…For what?"

She glanced over her shoulder, keeping her voice low.

"Only reason you'd be there is if you were hopping on a train."

Tomoe had found him at the JR gates. It was a bit off the path to the Odakyu Line or the Enoden, so only people taking the JR would pass through there.

"Like I'd have Christmas Eve plans," she grumbled. "Unlike you, I'm not dating anybody."

Christmas was evidently a sore point.

"Then why were you there?"

"……"

She turned sideways and gave him a searching look.

He hadn't meant much by the question, but her reaction suggested there was something to it.

"Well?"

"No reason," she said with a pout.

She let out a long sigh, and when the bus stopped at a red light, she stood up.

And sat down next to Sakuta.

When the bus pulled out again, she said, "Promise you won't laugh."

"I'd prefer a funny story, actually."

It felt like a long time since anything had made him laugh. There had been too many not-funny things happening one after another.

"Then I'm not telling."

"Don't be mean."

"You were mean first."

"No, I genuinely meant that."

"So you don't, usually?"

"You *are* fun to tease, Koga."

She sighed, giving up.

"I had a dream about you last night," she said reluctantly.

"You did?"

"You were at the station, in trouble. Calling out to everyone around you...but nobody was paying any attention. I couldn't make out what you were saying, but you sounded pretty desperate."

"......"

That was *exactly* what had happened before Tomoe found him.

"But it was a dream, right?"

"Sure, but...we had some weirdness over summer, remember?" she said.

"True."

That had been Tomoe's Adolescence Syndrome. Crazily enough, she'd generated a time loop that lasted until she got the future she desired. They'd concluded that she was just simulating the future in her dreams, but Sakuta had gotten pulled into that dream and been forced to loop with her.

"So this dream super bugged me."

"That's all?"

"I'd never seen you like that."

"……"

"I don't wanna see you crying and screaming."

"Yeah…"

Maybe what she'd seen was a future after her arrival. He'd certainly been getting pretty desperate, but not quite to the point of breaking down in tears. Tomoe had found him before that happened.

When Sakuta was caught up in Tomoe's Adolescence Syndrome, Rio had explained the concept of quantum entanglement. Something about two correlated quantum particles capable of exchanging information instantly regardless of distance.

And for those particles to become entangled, there had to be a powerful stimulus—at least, he had a vague recollection of something like that.

"Everyone needs someone you've exchanged butt kicks with."

"Seriously, forget that."

"Like I ever could."

"Force yourself."

"I especially remember when you said, 'Stronger!'"

"You're horrible."

She glared at him, her cheeks red. Her hands were clapped on her butt again, which made this not at all threatening.

"You're extra cute today, Koga."

"D-don't call me cute!"

As they laughed about that, Sakuta hit the button for the next stop.

They got off at the stop by the hospital where Shouko was staying. The white building was right in front of them.

"You need my help…at a hospital?"

"Yeah."

"We seeing someone here?"

She opened her umbrella and took a few steps forward...then stopped, realizing Sakuta was still at the bus stop.

"Senpai?" she said, turning around. She was already three yards away. "You aren't coming?"

"Koga."

"Mm?"

"I need a favor."

"...What?"

She'd picked up on his grim vibe and was taking this seriously.

"I need you to find the other me."

"......"

"......"

"Hurr?"

Tomoe let out a very dumb noise.

Several minutes later, Sakuta was in a small mall not far from the hospital. A supermarket, drugstore, bookstore, et cetera surrounded by a largish parking lot.

He was in a phone booth on the corner.

Standing by the phone, he checked the watch he'd borrowed from Tomoe. Before they split up, he'd promised to call her in ten minutes.

For one simple reason: so he could talk to this timeline's Sakuta—present Sakuta. He had to warn him of what the future held. Present Sakuta needed to know that his actions would cost Mai her life.

Meeting directly would be easier, but if he understood Rio's lecture correctly, it was impossible for future Sakuta and present Sakuta to meet face-to-face.

But he also knew of one exception. Last summer, during Rio's bout of Adolescence Syndrome. Rio had been split in two, but they'd been able to talk on the phone.

He checked the watch again. The ten minutes was up.

Sakuta lifted the receiver and dropped in a one-hundred-yen coin—also borrowed from Tomoe. He dialed her cell phone number from the note she'd given him.

A few moments after entering the tenth digit, he heard it ringing.

That alone was a relief.

"Senpai?" Tomoe's voice came on the line. She definitely sounded pretty rattled. And the reason for that was exactly why he was calling.

"Yeah, it's me."

"There really are two of you!"

As rattled as she was, he could tell she really wanted to shower him with questions. Knowing that this must be Adolescence Syndrome helped mitigate some of the unavoidable shock.

When Sakuta said nothing else, Tomoe prompted him. "Senpai?"

But answering her questions was more than he could handle now. Confronting his past self had his heart racing.

"Let me talk to the other me."

"...You'd better explain later."

He could tell she'd moved the phone away from her ear. He could hear voices talking on the other end. Probably trying in vain to explain what was happening to present Sakuta. A hopeless task.

But it wasn't long before he heard breathing on the line. Present Sakuta must have decided on the direct approach.

There was a brief intake of breath. Then...

"Are you really me?"

Was that really what Sakuta sounded like?

Present Sakuta wasn't even trying to hide his suspicion. He came across like a cocky asshole, but it wasn't like Sakuta didn't already know that about himself.

"Yep. I'm you from four days in the future," he said.

He could have started soft, eased himself into it—but he didn't feel like it.

"Four days?"

"Yep."

"But that means…"

"I know what's gonna happen today."

"……"

That sounded like a gulp.

"And that's why I'm here to change it."

"Wait."

Present Sakuta's voice was growing hostile.

Sakuta knew exactly why. If future Sakuta was actually from the future, that meant he'd survived. Present Sakuta had worked that out, and that led to the obvious question.

"I wasn't in an accident?" present Sakuta asked. Clearly stifling his emotions.

"No," Sakuta said.

"Then Makinohara…" His voice shook. He was obviously crest-fallen, certain he'd robbed her of her future.

"Don't worry. The transplant was a success."

"……?"

A wordless question, one conveyed through breaths alone.

"Even though I wasn't in an accident?" he asked slowly. Choosing his words.

"That's right." The reply was quiet.

"……"

"So there's no need for you to go to the scene."

"……That doesn't make sense."

He sounded calm. And very certain.

Present Sakuta knew that didn't add up. Even this short conversation had been more than enough to tell him that.

He'd hoped to avoid spelling it out. But that didn't seem like a viable option.

"If my future was a good one, would I have come back in time?" he asked.

"……"

"Someone else takes your place."

Even if Sakuta didn't say who, he was sure the possibility was crossing present Sakuta's mind. And the eerie calm in his voice proved it.

"Who?"

It was less a question than a confirmation. Checking to see if his answer was right. Possibly hoping it would be wrong.

But future Sakuta could not answer present Sakuta's plea. Only convey the truth.

"Mai."

Just saying it aloud brought back those memories. An invisible force made his body creak. He could barely breathe. He gasped, desperate for oxygen but finding none.

All he could do was clutch his hand to his chest, waiting for the wave of pain and grief to wash over him.

"What...?"

"......"

"What did I do wrong?"

"Just before the van hit, Mai pushed me out of the way."

"......"

"That's how I survived."

"......"

Present Sakuta had yet to experience any of this, but it still left him speechless. What look was on his face, Sakuta couldn't guess. It was hard to imagine your own expressions, and trying seemed pointless, so he quickly abandoned the attempt.

"I survived because of Mai," he said, making the facts crystal clear.

This was the future. This would happen. At six o'clock on December 24.

"So...what?" present Sakuta spluttered.

Having gone down this road himself, Sakuta knew what it was like to place lives on the scales. Sacrifice himself to save Shouko? Or survive into a future with Mai?

He'd had two options.

And had been forced to choose one.

He'd racked his brain until he was sick of thinking about it—and now here was future Sakuta, showing up at the last minute with a third potential outcome. It was no small task to grasp the concept, accept the truth of it, and sort through his feelings. Having to rethink the whole thing at this stage would make him want to insist it couldn't be true.

And there would be no way of knowing what the right choice was.

"……"

Present Sakuta said nothing. Most likely, he wasn't even capable of thought.

But future Sakuta was different. He'd already thought this through and found his answer. And because he'd made his choice, he'd come back in time. To force that path.

"I'm here to save Mai."

"……"

"So don't you dare go to meet her."

"…But…"

"If you go, it'll be Mai who dies."

"!"

"If you go to the aquarium, Mai will die."

As he said the words, tears began to flow. Halfway through the line, his voice broke, choked with tears. But he wasn't about to stay quiet long enough for those emotions to subside.

"And I'm not going through that again!"

He had to get these feelings across somehow. He needed present Sakuta to know just how bad it was.

"Losing Mai…is *not* an option."

"……But if I don't go, what happens to Makinohara?!"

The obvious question. The emotions behind it were every bit as intense.

"……"

But Sakuta didn't have an answer. And that silence spoke volumes.

"What are you doing?"

"I made my choice."

"You're me. How can you do this?" His voice low. He must have realized what Sakuta was doing. "You want me to give up on her?"

His tone was cold. Contemptuous. Outright refuting and rebuking Sakuta.

"You don't care what happens to Makinohara?!"

"Of course I do!"

He definitely cared. He meant that. But he knew he had to make a choice. Having gone through Mai's death, future Sakuta knew what choice he had to make.

"You saw her, too. Makinohara, lying in that ICU. Clinging to life."

"……"

"Everything she's been through…trying not to worry anyone, hiding her own suffering, keeping her fears hidden. Always smiling when she was with you."

"……"

"And you don't give a damn about any of that? You're willing to just let that all go to waste?"

That low hiss was hitting Sakuta hard, ripping into him. Aiming right where it hurt the most.

His knuckles tightened on the receiver, but his expression never changed.

He'd made his choice.

And had come from the future to achieve it.

"I want to make Mai happy."

"That's not an answer!"

"I can't do anything for Makinohara."

"! Are…are you really me?!"

"I am."

"You've lost it."

There was nothing left but scorn.

"Maybe."

"You've gone mad."

Irritation and contempt.

"I can live with that."

"……"

Sakuta didn't waver, and that finally silenced his counterpart.

"If I live and can make Mai happy…that's enough."

"How can you say that?! I'd rather get run over than stand by while Makinohara dies! That's what's supposed to happen!"

"Even if it makes Mai cry?"

"! Just make sure you stop her."

And with that, he hung up.

The phone on his ear, Sakuta muttered, "I'm so pigheaded."

What a difference four days made. Back then, he'd have made the same choice. The events of December 24 had permanently changed him.

He put the phone down. Then he picked it up and called the same number again.

"Oh, senpai?" Tomoe answered.

"What's up with the other me?"

"Dunno. He ran off somewhere," she said. "What's going on?"

"It's what it looks like."

"I'm asking 'cause looking didn't help!"

"Something came up, and now there's two of me. Happens all the time."

"It does not!"

"Really?"

The causes were different, but between Rio, Shouko, and himself, this was already Sakuta's third experience with it. Anything happening that often couldn't really be called uncommon anymore.

"And is it really you I'm talking to, senpai?"

"Oh, that reminds me. Make sure that guy pays you back the three thousand yen I borrowed."

"Never mind, it's definitely you."

He wasn't sure why that was what convinced her, but at least she believed him.

"It's Adolescence Syndrome, right?" she asked, lowering her voice.

"Well, yeah."

"Anything I can do?"

"You've already bailed me out big-time."

Honestly, it had never occurred to him it would be Tomoe who came to his rescue.

"But there's still two of you! And you're still wrestling with something serious, right?"

"I've got a plan there—don't worry."

"……"

He didn't need any help to picture the disgruntled look on her face.

"No pouting."

"I'm not pouting!"

She most certainly was.

"Mkay, let me ask you for one other thing."

"Okay, what?"

"If you see me tomorrow or after that…just be yourself."

"……Sure."

She might not fully understand, but Sakuta's earnest tone had made an impression on her. Tomoe had answered in kind.

"It'll help a lot if I can just harass you like always."

"I oughtta press charges."

"That's the spirit."

"I'm legitimately worried here!"

This made him laugh out loud. He hadn't done that in a while.

He wasn't trying to keep secrets from her. Once this was all over, he planned to tell her what he could. But until it was over—specifically after six PM—he couldn't be sure what would happen to him. He didn't want to make any promises.

Sakuta had been to the future because of present Sakuta's Adolescence Syndrome. What would happen to future Sakuta if that was resolved? Would he go back to the future? Or would he and his future cease to exist? He didn't know. He couldn't say for sure until it happened.

"Well, I'm not exactly happy about it, but okay. Senpai, you're pressed for time, right?"

"Yeah."

"Then we'll talk later."

"Yep. Later."

Yet here he was agreeing to talk again. He laughed at himself as he put the receiver down. Then he remembered he wasn't done yet and picked the phone up again.

He had to pull this number out of the depths of his memory.

He punched in all eleven digits, then let the air out of his lungs.

He put the receiver to his ear, listening to it ring.

"C'mon, pick up," he muttered.

It was an obvious sign that he was stressing out about this.

It rang five times.

"……"

Still no answer.

Seven rings. It might send him to voice mail any second now. But before it did, the ring cut off. The call went through.

"Yeah?"

A girl answered, keeping her voice down, clearly on guard. The call would have come up as a public phone.

But she'd answered anyway—because she knew someone who used those all the time.

"It's me. Sakuta."

"I figured," she said, her voice back to normal. If slightly annoyed. "What?" she asked.

This was Nodoka.

"Sorry. Busy prepping for your concert?"

Nodoka was part of an idol group called Sweet Bullet, and he knew they had a Christmas show.

"Just finished rehearsal. I'm on break, so…what is it?"

"Any idea where Mai is right now?"

"At the TV station. Filming interiors."

"I was wondering where that station is."

"Huh?"

"Wanted to go see her."

Might as well be direct.

"They aren't gonna let you in if you just roll up there," she said.

Like she thought he was an idiot.

"Are you completely stupid?"

She also said it out loud.

"I mean, that's why I'm asking you."

"Huh? You call this asking?"

"Please."

"......"

"Seriously, please. I wanna surprise her."

He dug in. There would be no backing down.

"...What happened Sunday?" Nodoka asked, answering with a question. "After Kaede's haircut...something went down between the two of you."

"......"

He remembered. Like Nodoka said, they'd all gone out together to take Kaede to a hair salon. On the way home, Sakuta and Mai had split off. They'd taken a train away from home, down the Tokaido Line, all the way to Atami. Mai had cried a lot there.

Until that moment, Sakuta had been ready to sacrifice himself if it meant saving Shouko. But Mai's tears had left his head spinning. Seeing her cry had shaken his resolve.

For the first time, he wanted to live.

The need had never felt so great.

He knew he never wanted to make Mai cry like that again.

But he hadn't managed to tell her that. He couldn't bring himself to say something that awful. Awful because that meant abandoning Shouko to her fate.

"She got back late and...went straight to her room. She didn't say a word to me."

"Mm."

"Don't just grunt at me!"

"I figure you'll wind up punching me for it."

"Oh?" She was growling already. "Where are you, Sakuta?"

"Fujisawa. By the hospital."

"Get your butt to Shinbashi."

He looked at the watch.

"That'll take an hour."

"Not if you hop on an express. Four o'clock at JR Karasumori Exit. Shiodome side."

"Huh? But don't you have a show?"

"I got time before it starts, and apparently, I gotta punch you first."

"Wow. Now I don't wanna go."

"And I haven't picked a Christmas present for her yet anyway. I'm not doing this for you, got that?"

"Don't worry—nothing you've said could *possibly* give me that idea."

"See you at four."

"Got it. On my way."

He repeated *Shinbashi, Karasumori Exit, Shiodome side* and hung up. He gathered up the row of coins and left the phone booth.

4

Sakuta headed back to Fujisawa Station and got on a JR Tokaido Line train. An express bound for Koganei. He double-checked the map of the line on the screen above the doors. Six stops between here and Shinbashi. It would take him forty-one minutes. Nodoka was right; it would be less than an hour. Now he just had to pray the snow didn't cause any delays. There were none showing right now.

"Mommy! There's a bunny man!"

On the way, a little girl got on the train and pointed at Sakuta. He was still wearing that costume. The head was in his hands—it had been too big to fit in the luggage racks.

This had drawn a lot of attention and not just from the little girl. Same thing on his way through the gates at Fujisawa and while waiting for the train to arrive.

Now that Tomoe had made it possible for people to see him, there was no real need to keep wearing the bunny outfit, but emotionally, he wasn't prepared to leave it behind.

What if people stopped perceiving him again?

He couldn't quite shake that fear.

And that left him wanting to stick out no matter how many weird looks he got. He wanted a reminder that people could see him.

Fortunately, it *was* December 24.

Everyone looking at him went, "Well, it *is* Christmas." He'd passed a police officer on patrol at Fujisawa without being asked any questions. Maybe they'd just assumed he was on break from a job at a cake shop. He'd seen Santas and reindeer running around the department stores by Fujisawa, so it wasn't all that odd to assume there was a bunny among them.

"Bye-bye, bunny man!"

The little girl and her mom got off one stop before his destination.

He waved back. Figured it couldn't hurt to let everyone know he was harmless. He definitely didn't want to get labeled suspicious and have someone report him.

While he worried about that, the train reached Shinbashi Station.

He was off the train before the doors were fully open.

He checked the signs in front of him, searching for the exit Nodoka had specified. Hibiya Exit, Ginza Exit, Shiodome Exit—there sure were a lot of exits. And the Karasumori Exit was, confusingly, split in two, with one side labeled FOR SHIODOME and the other FOR KARASUMORI.

"So that's what Toyohama meant?"

He'd wondered why she specified a side after the exit name. It all made sense now that he was here.

He followed the arrows, hastening to the meeting location. The clocks on the platform said it was almost four.

Down the stairs, he saw Nodoka waiting just outside the gates.

He ran his ticket through the machine and was out.

She ran up to him as he exited. Underneath her duffle coat, he could see a T-shirt poking out from underneath—yellow, Nodoka's color. That was definitely a Sweet Bullet logo on it.

It was right before a concert, so her makeup was extra intense. Which really enhanced the glare she gave him.

"You have *got* to be kidding me."

Obviously, she was referring to his outfit.

"This is the result of serious reflection on a problem I was having."

What he said was true. He meant every word. The problem was just insanely complicated and would take forever to explain.

"But I guess it shortcuts a few things," Nodoka said, before he could find the words.

"What do you mean?"

"Just follow me."

She stalked away.

Shrugging, he went after her.

Figuring it was best not to tempt fate, he didn't mention the punch she'd promised him.

There was a familiar vehicle parked outside the station. A white mini-van. The same type driven by Mai's manager, Ryouko Hanawa.

And while that thought was crossing his mind, he saw Ryouko sitting in the driver's seat.

"Get in," Nodoka said, opening the back door. "All the way." She pushed him inside and climbed in after.

"You talked to her manager?" he said.

He assumed that was why she was here.

"Even I can't just waltz into a TV studio if I'm not filming there. Good thing I got Ryouko's number in case anything came up."

"I didn't give it to you for things like this," Ryouko said, glaring at them in the mirror.

"Sorry," Sakuta said.

"I'll help this time, but…try not to fight in the first place."

Their eyes met in the mirror. A reminder that this was the second time. He'd forced her to help him out up in Kanazawa, for Mai's birthday. That certainly left him without a leg to stand on.

"Sorry," he said again.

When Ryouko said nothing further, he turned to Nodoka.

"Is the studio far?" he asked. His time was limited. He hoped it was close.

"That's it," she said, pointing at the building right next to them. A huge building that had been in his line of sight since he stepped out of the station.

"Huh?" he said. It was, like, a minute or two from the station on foot.

And the roads themselves were stupid busy, so driving would probably take *more* time. They'd already been moving for three minutes and were only just turning into the garage.

"Sakuta, put your head on," Nodoka said. She reached out and helped.

It was very hard to see now. He could only make out a narrow range through the holes in the costume's nose. The van rolled into the garage and stopped by the security gate.

"Talent for a shoot," Ryouko said, showing the badge around her neck to the uniformed guard.

"Okay. Have a good one."

Ryouko nodded back, and the gate went up. The car pulled out, and Sakuta bobbed his head at the guard in passing. The car drove to the back of the lot.

"It's easier to get things past security here than at the main entrance upstairs," Ryouko explained once they were parked. That was why she'd gone to the trouble of driving him.

He followed Nodoka out of the van. It was hard moving around with the head on. He reached up to take it off, but Ryouko stopped him.

"Leave it on," she said. "I don't want a media circus because her boyfriend showed up at the studio."

She was keeping her voice down, but she'd made her point loud and clear.

He nodded, in complete agreement. This must have been the plan from the start. That explained why there was a reindeer costume on the third row of seats in the van. Why Nodoka had called it a shortcut.

"It's just kinda hard to walk."

He could only see a small range in front of him. Nothing to either side, and there was no guarantee he could avoid bumping into things.

"I'll escort you, then," Nodoka said, hooking her arm around his right. "C'mon."

She started dragging him along.

"Have you told Mai I'm coming?"

Mindful of Ryouko's warning, he kept his voice low.

He'd been asking Nodoka, but Ryouko said, "No. She was filming when the call came in. She should be done and in the green room by now."

They must have boarded the elevators. He couldn't really see, but he felt the sudden rise.

The elevator made several stops. TV staff flooded on and off. He didn't see anyone especially famous.

By the time the bell rang for their stop, it was just the three of them.

"Here we are," Nodoka said. When the doors opened, she gave him a tug, and they stepped out. He did a little shuffle, trying to look around.

A long corridor stretched in both directions. Doors placed at regular intervals. Names of the talent within next to each.

He saw Mai Sakurajima on a door ten yards down the hall.

"......!"

He tensed up.

Mai was here.

Just a door between them.

Mai. Alive.

Just the thought was making him tremble.

"Sakuta?"

Nodoka must have felt him shaking.

Before he could answer, Ryouko knocked on Mai's door.

"It's Hanawa. Okay to enter?"

"Yes, go ahead."

Mai's voice, through the door.

He knew it.

He'd recognize it anywhere.

The sound waves rippled through him. He could feel her presence.

That was Mai.

She was really here.

"……"

He'd meant to whisper her name, but no sound emerged.

Ryouko opened the green room door.

"Good work today," she said as she crossed the threshold.

"Thanks, Ryouko. You too."

"I've brought some company."

"Company?"

Nodoka went in next.

"Nodoka! What brings you here?"

"I've got a Christmas present for you."

Nodoka pulled his arm, and Sakuta stepped into the room. Ryouko quickly slipped around behind him; then he heard the door click shut.

He adjusted the costume's narrow field of view until he had Mai in his sights, there on the other side of that little hole. Standing there, alive.

Mai was looking at him. In his direction.

"……?"

Half confused, half puzzled. But she wasn't looking away. Her eyes locked onto a costume that wasn't saying anything.

He wanted to cry out. He thought about pulling the head off and revealing himself.

But he couldn't do either right now.

And only he knew why.

He wasn't even sure when the first drop had fallen. The levees had long since broken, and there was nothing he could do to stop the waterworks.

"......"

He had things to tell her but couldn't bring himself to start. If he said anything, his voice would be choked with tears, and she'd know he was crying.

Every cell in his body was shaking with joy from the simple fact that Mai was alive. Sobbing with delight. All he could do was ride the rapids of emotion. Simply wait for the deluge to pass.

"Thank you, Nodoka," Mai said, turning away. "And, Ryouko, sorry to rope you into this again. I can handle the rest. Can you give us a moment together?"

It sounded like she'd guessed something was up, which was a huge relief.

Sakuta didn't recognize the scent in the green room. There was a huge mirror with a vast array of makeup before it. Costumes for the shoot hung from the rack behind them. All of that combined with the kind of perfume grown-ups wore left a sweet lingering fragrance.

The room itself was fairly big, maybe 180 square feet. Half of that was an elevated tatami floor.

Sakuta was sitting on the edge of that, still in the bunny costume. The head was still on. He was just waiting for the shaking to subside.

After a minute, the door opened from the outside.

Mai had walked Nodoka to the elevator and come back to him.

She closed the door behind her.

Her eyes locked on him.

"How long are you gonna sit there?" she asked.

He shook his head once, an attempt at an answer. He still couldn't speak without revealing his tears.

"Did you come here to sit in silence?"

Her footsteps came closer.

He had his head down, and her feet came into view. They stopped in front of him.

"That's not why you came back from the future, is it?"

"?!"

"Are you planning on making me do *all* the work?"

"Mai…"

His head went up. And his narrow, dark field of view was filled with light. Mai had pulled the head off his costume.

Mai was right there in front of him.

He could see her clearly now.

She was smiling at him.

"It's really you," he said. A whole new wave of tears came pouring out. Between the tears and the sweat, his face must have been a mess. But she reached out her hands to him, wrapped them around his head, and drew him to her chest.

"Mai……?"

"Good," she said. He didn't know what that meant. "I was able to save you."

"……"

Her words went right to the heart of the matter, and it wasn't like that didn't come as a surprise. But he also knew right away that she already knew everything.

"Good," she said again.

"…It's not good at all, Mai." His voice broke. His nose was clogged. "It's my fault you…"

"I was finally able to do something for you."

"……!"

He couldn't put his feelings into words, but he wanted to refute that, so he shook his head like a toddler throwing a tantrum.

"I never thought you'd do that," he managed.

"I told you. I love you a lot more than you think I do."

Her arms tightened around his head. In her embrace, he could distinctly feel her heart beating. Proof she was alive. The pulse of life.

Right here, right now, Mai's mind was already made up.

He should have known that, but only with her warmth around him did realization set in. No matter what, she would save him. That was Mai's decision.

"I'm sorry, Sakuta."

Her voice was gentle.

"Why are *you* apologizing?"

"I made you cry like this."

"I…"

"I left you alone."

"…I…I just…"

He couldn't say more, couldn't think of anything else to say. His feelings for her couldn't be expressed in words, only tears.

Here in her arms, every part of him could feel Mai. Her breath in his ear brought him peace. Her feelings for him reached his very heart.

He was no longer trying to stop crying. Mai had given him these tears. So he clung to her, letting them out, like he was returning the feeling.

But they couldn't stay like this forever.

Sakuta had things to do.

And so did Mai.

"Sakuta," she said, pulling back. "Let me see your face."

She cupped it in both hands. He looked up at her.

"You haven't grown much," she said, a little choked up herself.

"I'm from the future, but only four days."

"Oh. I got a voice mail from Sakuta saying there was a future you around, so I got all excited."

"I'll grow up eventually, but you'll have to wait for that to happen."

Mai's smile seemed slightly conflicted.

"I've gotta go."

"Go…?"

"We've got a date, remember?"

She took a coat off the rack. She was already headed for the door.

"Wait, Mai."

He stood up and grabbed her arm.

"Let go."

She spoke quietly but she held firm.

"It'll be okay," he said.

"Like hell it will!" she snapped. She spun toward him, tears in her eyes. "If Sakuta knows I'll be in the accident, that'll just make him want to sacrifice himself even more! He'll just take that as proof he should be the one to die!"

"……"

"He would *never* agree to live at the cost of the two Shoukos' futures."

He knew full well how right she was. Mai understood him completely.

"If I don't go, Sakuta's gonna die!"

She understood him, but not this version of him. She didn't know future Sakuta. She didn't get what losing her had done to him.

"Let go!"

She tried to shake him off, but he pulled her close, wrapping his arms around her from behind.

"Please, Mai. Stay here."

He tightened his grip, not letting her get away.

"Please…"

But his voice was barely a whisper.

He knew he was shaking like a leaf.

Trembling. A complete mess.

"…Sakuta?"

He was trying to hold her tight, but there was barely any strength to it. And that, in turn, made her stop fighting him.

"I can't…I can't lose you again."

The shaking wouldn't stop. He was shaking so hard his heels were lifting off the floor.

"Stay here until after six."

"But…"

"It'll be okay."

"……"

"I'll do something about me."

He knew that didn't sound convincing.

He was still trembling pathetically.

The fear was overwhelming.

He was scared of losing Mai.

Scared to the bone.

And he was afraid of what he was about to attempt.

After all, it meant stealing Shouko's future.

"You're really fine with that?" Mai asked, stifling her own feelings.

He nodded wordlessly. "I made up my mind."

His voice was a croak. Barely containing the emotions.

"So I need you to wait here."

"......"

Mai was still hesitating. He could hear it in her breath.

"I mean, it's me we're talking about, so I'm sure I'll come back to you in tears."

"...Sakuta."

"And I'll need your arms around me again."

"You're sure?"

"You'll help me get through it."

"Sakuta..."

"And I'll make you happy."

"......"

Sakuta heard her sniff. He slipped a key into her hand. The key to his apartment. The one he'd taken from the mailbox.

"Take this. Please."

"......Okay," she whispered. Clutching the key tight.

"Thank you, Mai."

"But you've got one thing wrong, Sakuta."

She turned in his arms and faced him. Her forehead tapped his.

"I don't need you to make me happy."

"......Huh?"

"We'll be happy together. You and me."

Mai's words hit him right in the heart. Then he felt her presence within him, spreading outward through every fiber of his being. A warmth, like the spring sun. He felt sure moments like this were what "happiness" was all about.

"I knew it," he said, his lips curling up in a smile.

"Knew what?" She scowled at him.

"I'll never be a match for you, Mai."

With just one line, she'd stopped his trembling.

They'd be happy *together*.

Armed with those words, he might still have doubts and worries, but he knew in the end he'd find his way. If their thoughts were aligned, it would all work out.

With some reluctance, Sakuta let Mai go. He felt if he clung to her any longer, he'd never leave. He'd want to feel her presence forever.

But Sakuta had to go.

Back out into the falling snow.

"I'll be waiting for you, Sakuta."

"I know."

Mai had put her faith in him, and he had to keep that promise.

"I'll be waiting—so make sure you come home to me."

"I will."

And to keep that promise, he had to leave her side.

"Go on, Sakuta."

"See you soon, Mai."

5

When Sakuta left Mai's green room, he found her manager on standby in the hall and got her to give him a ride back to Shinbashi Station. He traveled in full bunny costume to avoid any unexpected media attention, of course.

At the station, he boarded a train back the way he'd come. An Atami-bound train on the JR Tokaido Line.

Forty-five minutes rocking in a bunny costume. He got off at his home station (Fujisawa) and switched to the Odakyu Enoshima Line.

The train pulled out of the reversing station, the shopping district streaming past outside the windows. The view soon switched to a quiet residential area. All the houses were covered in a light dusting of snow. Sakuta watched them go by as the train stopped in Hon-Kugenuma and Kugenuma Beach. Then it reached the end of the line—Katase-Enoshima Station.

Parts of the platform weren't covered, and there was an inch of snow piled up. A little boy was happily stomping around in the untouched snow, leaving footprints behind.

He checked the time on the station clock. Not quite five thirty.

Thirty minutes till the accident.

He ran his ticket through the gate and left the station.

The flow of the crowd parted outside. One stream headed right, toward the aquarium, and the other went straight in the direction of the Benten Bridge and Enoshima.

Unlike the first December 24, Sakuta didn't turn toward the aquarium. He took the road down to Benten Bridge.

Despite the swirling snow, the road was jam-packed. College couples sharing umbrellas and families with young kids excited about the snow filled the streets. Nobody was grumbling about it. They welcomed the lively atmosphere with open arms—it was the holy night, after all. The snow only made it all better.

This was a coastal town where snow almost never stuck. And it had been years since it last snowed on Christmas Eve. Everyone was thrilled.

Sakuta was pushing through the crowd, umbrellaless.

He could feel his heart racing as he neared the scene of the accident. He could feel the stress mounting. His feet were getting wobbly.

He hadn't been back here since it happened.

All it would do was remind him of Mai lying there, bathed in streetlights.

His instincts were screaming at him not to go.

But here he was.

There were things he could do only here. Things he had to do.

But it was still a little early for that.

"……"

Honestly, he wasn't sure if he should be doing this. But because he wasn't sure, he moved away from the accident location and headed into the underground walkway that led to the other side of Route 134. This tunnel had been designed to keep a steady flow of pedestrian traffic moving under the busy main drag, pumping tourists onto the Benten Bridge and Enoshima beyond.

Sakuta came up the other side and found himself just in front of the bridge.

Most people headed straight across to the island. Sakuta alone peeled off from the crowd.

He stopped by the two dragon lanterns.

This was where he'd agreed to meet big Shouko four days ago—by future Sakuta's time scale—on the first December 24.

She wasn't here yet. That was a bit of a relief. Despite the cold, he could tell his brow was damp with sweat.

Walking around in this costume was wearing him out.

By way of taking a break, he undid the zipper and freed his arms and upper body. He had his school tracksuit on underneath. He sat down on the curb by the lantern, the head resting on his knees, cradled against his chest.

Any number of couples passed him by. All here to see the illumination on the Sea Candle, the lighthouse at the top of Enoshima. You could see the glow clearly from here. At the top, it was like a garden of lights at your feet.

Everyone was giving the boy in the bunny suit funny looks, but the lights quickly stole their attention away.

Only one person stopped.

She looked surprised to see Sakuta there, and her mind was obviously racing. But when she reached him, she had her usual calm smile again.

"I keep you waiting?"

"Not at all. It's not even time yet."

"You were so excited about a date with me you came early!"

"Totally."

He just admitted it. He wasn't here to play word games.

"You certainly have an unusual way of dressing up for the big date," she said with a laugh, looking over his costume.

"I've been wearing it all day. It's a part of me now."

Shouko was wearing a pretty standard outfit for her. A bulky sweater and a long skirt. She had a shawl over her shoulders but, like Sakuta, no umbrella.

She reached out and touched his head.

"You've got snow on you," she said, brushing it away. "Sorry."

He glanced up to ask why and saw sadness in her eyes. So he didn't ask.

"I messed up, huh?" she said.

He didn't need her to spell out what she meant.

"I wouldn't say that."

"But here you are. From the future."

She got right to the point. That explained everything. She already knew. She might not know what future he'd seen, but she knew it was bad enough he'd had to come back. Just like she had.

"......"

He just shook his head.

She hadn't messed up.

"I'm here because of you."

This was true.

The feelings behind it were, too.

Because she'd told him what lay ahead.

Because she'd tried to save him.

Because she'd given him a chance to choose.

That was what led to this.

That was what brought Sakuta here.

With his choice made.

She'd done the same, two years before.

Since their first meeting on the beach at Shichirigahama, Shouko hadn't changed.

She'd been a source of support and the object of his aspiration.

He wanted to be there for others like she was for him. He'd lived with that goal ever since. He wanted to be like that for someone. Even if it was only one person.

He still hadn't managed that, but he *had* found his one. The one he had to protect, no matter the cost. The one he wanted to make happy. The one he wanted to share his life with.

If he'd never met Shouko, he didn't think he'd ever have figured that out.

Shouko had taught him everything that mattered.

"Thank you" wasn't enough to express his gratitude.

"Sorry" wasn't enough to convey the pain he felt.

What should he say in a moment like this?

Sakuta still wasn't sure. Shouko hadn't taught him that yet.

But of course he didn't know. Of course she hadn't taught him. You could search the whole world over, and you'd never find a word that spoke such volumes.

Yet he still opened his mouth to try and tell her *something*.

"Shouko, I…"

But nothing else came. He couldn't find the words.

He didn't know what to say. The thoughts were right there, swirling around inside him. He was overflowing with emotion, but there was no way for them to get out.

Shouko took one look at him, smiled, and said, "Sakuta. Hold my hand."

He hadn't seen that coming.

She held her hand out, and he took it.

He could feel her presence on his palm. Each finger confirming she was real.

"This is pretty embarrassing," she said, her smile getting shifty. She glanced briefly at him, then at Enoshima.

The Sea Candle illumination lit up the snow falling from the night sky.

Sakuta, too, turned his gaze to the lights.

The sea breeze was chilly in winter.

His body was becoming numb. Only the heat of Shouko's palm on his reminded him he was really there.

She gave his hand a little squeeze.

"......"

He could tell she was anxious.

So he squeezed back. That just made her squeeze even harder. But her grip no longer felt anxious.

There was a strength to it that felt like she was encouraging him. She held on tight, like she was rooting for him, for the future he was trying to carve out.

After a minute, she relaxed her grip. She swung their clasped hands gently back and forth. They must have seemed like a couple goofing around. Neither anxious nor encouraging. This was your classic Shouko tease.

Holding hands had conveyed more than words ever could.

He was pretty sure she'd grasped what he was feeling, too.

So he spoke to her one more time.

"Shouko."

He just had to do the best he could with the words he had. But as clumsy as that might be, he felt it would be enough.

"......"

Shouko said nothing. But he knew she was listening.

"I'll take everything with me."

"......"

"I'll take it all into the future."

"......"

"My time spent with you, everything you gave me...everything Makinohara worked for, and my memories of it. I won't leave anything behind. It'll stay with me in the future."

"......"

Shouko gently shook her head.

"Sakuta, do you know why it is people forget things?"

"I won't forget."

"I know why. It's because there are things they want to forget."

"......"

"Nothing's worse than painful memories that last forever."

"All the more reason I won't forget you."

"...How's that?"

"My memories of you are the bittersweet memories of a first love. Why would I need to forget that?"

"Seriously."

Her tone was loaded, but she stopped without saying more.

Sakuta turned toward her, curious.

"You're such a jerk," she said with a smile.

He didn't respond. He could tell she didn't want him to.

Both of them looked straight ahead.

Across the long bridge to Enoshima.

A tiny island, floating on the ocean.

And at the top, a world of light in a crystal made of snow.

All he wanted to do right now was remember seeing this with Shouko. To remember how her hand felt in his.

They couldn't stay like this for long.

Sakuta still had things to do.

And their brief time together soon came to an end.

"I've gotta get moving," he said.

It was admittedly a bit reluctant. But there was no hesitation.

"Okay," Shouko said. She let go of his hand.

Sakuta put his costume back on, and Shouko helped him with the zipper in the back.

Holding the head, he turned to face her once again.

He'd come here to tell her something, but he found himself at a loss for words.

So he looked her in the eye and said, "Good-bye, Shouko."

For an instant, her eyes clouded. But she kept her smile going.

"Bye, Sakuta."

She gave him a little wave.

Sakuta turned and walked away. He knew Shouko was still waving. He was absolutely certain of it, but he didn't turn back.

Each step he took felt like he had to peel his foot off the ground. He headed through the tunnel under Route 134 to the other side.

It was almost six.

When he was in sight of the accident scene, he put the bunny costume's head on.

The Sakuta from the future could never meet the present-day Sakuta. It was impossible for both to be perceived in the same space at the same time.

But if you flipped that idea, both could coexist as long as they weren't observed. This was the principle that had allowed him to talk to present Sakuta on the phone.

So he just had to create a situation where people couldn't tell who he was.

Like the cat in a box, trapped in a state between life and death. It might be Sakuta in this costume; it might not be.

As Sakuta held his breath inside the costume, he heard someone panting. Ragged breathing, coming closer. And this proved his plan was working.

Present Sakuta was running across the thin dusting of snow, racing against time. Sakuta could see him clearly through the holes in the costume's nose. Himself, in his school uniform.

Trying to keep himself away from the accident location, he'd deliberately led present Sakuta toward the aquarium, but clearly, that ruse had not held up for long.

Present Sakuta was looking across the street at the dragon lanterns. His head went up. He must have found Shouko.

At the same time, a car horn blared. Costumed Sakuta was already on the move.

The black minivan braked hard, and the tires spun out. The car in front of it had slowed abruptly, and the minivan had almost hit it.

But once the tires lost their traction, the car was completely out of control.

"Sakuta!" Shouko screamed.

Present Sakuta saw the van coming and froze. But the look on his face was one of peace.

Naturally. He was convinced that sacrificing himself was the best choice.

Sakuta knew because he'd thought that himself.

If he could guarantee Shouko a future, then that was what he'd wanted—and as long as Mai didn't take his place, then this accident was how things should be.

But having lost Mai once... Memories of that grief had forced Sakuta to make a different choice.

He had to survive and make Mai happy. There was nothing for him except being happy with Mai.

People saw the van sliding toward them and screamed. It all seemed so far away to him. But his body kept moving with clear purpose. His goal simple.

Present Sakuta stood stock-still in the path of the skidding van— until future Sakuta, in a bunny costume, knocked him out of the way.

6

He felt someone shove him aside.

And felt himself shove someone.

Then he felt cold against his palms. Right and left.

Sakuta opened his eyes and saw his hands on the snow-covered asphalt. Going numb from the cold.

"Am I...?"

Not sure what was going on, he slowly peeled himself off the ground. Everything felt very wrong. The tension in the air was palpable.

The blare of the car horn filled the air.

He turned toward the sound and saw a black minivan resting against a toppled street sign. The front of it had caved in from the impact with the pole.

The crowd seemed stunned. It swelled as people stopped to see what had happened. Everyone was looking at the van and whispering to each other.

"Are you injured? Does it hurt anywhere?"

Dazed, Sakuta turned to find a young police officer talking to him. There was a police box nearby, and he must have come running. There was another, older officer on his radio, calling in the incident.

"Is this yours?" the officer asked, holding up the head of the bunny costume. The rest of the suit was lying at Sakuta's feet.

Both parts were empty. There was nothing inside.

A few moments ago, Sakuta had been wearing that suit. Those memories remained within him. But at the same time, he had another set of memories and sensations—and this set was very confused.

"Oh...so...," he muttered.

From the get-go, future Sakuta had been a creation of present Sakuta's Adolescence Syndrome. Unable to decide between Shouko's future or a future with Mai, his mind had succumbed to the pressure, and he'd rejected the future itself, hoping the moment of the accident would never arrive. And that desire had slowed down the world he perceived. If he took Rio at her word, the faster things moved, the slower time passed for them. As a result, the Sakuta who rejected the future wound up learning what would happen first.

But now that the cause of this Adolescence Syndrome was eliminated, the split in Sakuta's consciousness had merged. After six on December 24, there was no longer a need to choose between Shouko's future and his future with Mai.

The empty costume told him all of this, and his memories and sensations melted together. The separation between the two Sakutas faded away. They were both Sakuta. There was no real or fake. He was simply himself again.

"There's an ambulance on the way. You should get yourself checked out," the officer said, looking concerned.

"I'm fine," Sakuta said, and he turned to walk away.

The officer called after him, worried, but Sakuta did not respond.

He went through the tunnel again and stopped by the dragon lanterns. Looking from one lantern to the other.

"......"

This did not make Shouko appear.

Big Shouko was no longer around.

Sakuta had stolen her future.

And he had done it willingly.

He'd spent all day running around to make that happen.

And having achieved the result he wanted, he felt no sense of triumph, no elation of any kind. There was only pain in his chest.

The pain was so great he couldn't bear to stop moving. As if trying to get away from it, he started trudging toward Enoshima.

Benten Bridge stretched across the ocean's surface. It was over four hundred yards long, straight and level. Sakuta walked alone across it.

The nighttime sea was groaning below. It sounded like someone grieving.

There was a heat rising up inside him, behind his eyes. The back of his nose ached. But he was desperately keeping the tears at bay, moving one step at a time, uncertain where he was even trying to go. He just kept putting one foot in front of the other.

Feeling like this would eventually take him somewhere.

He crossed the whole bridge.

This brought him onto Enoshima proper.

Sakuta didn't stop there. He just kept plodding along.

Straight up the hill past the row of shops, through Enoshima Shrine, up the long set of stairs. One step after another.

His breathing grew ragged.

His legs were screaming at him.

But he didn't stop to rest. He had to be somewhere not here.

With each step he asked himself…

Was this okay?

Was this right?

Was it wrong?

Was there really no other way?

One bewildering question after another.

And he answered each out loud.

"No. There was no other way."

He gritted his teeth and put his foot on the next stair.

"Of course it isn't right. Look at what I did."

Another stair.

"It's all wrong."

The tears he'd been holding back were falling on his knees.

"It's not okay at all… None of this is okay."

He sniffed, wiped his eyes, and took another step.

There was nothing good about this.

A good outcome would be one where Shouko had a future, Sakuta was safe, and Mai was also alive. A future where all of them could smile. That was what he'd wanted.

He hadn't wanted *this*.

But it didn't matter what he'd wanted. This had been his only option. There was no outcome where everyone was happy. No magic trick could pull that off.

All Sakuta could do was choose Mai. And not Shouko.

"But that…doesn't make it okay. So don't god damn ask…"

He gnashed his teeth and forced himself up the last step.

He was staggering, out of breath just as he reached the base of the Sea Candle.

It was a tunnel of lights, like a wisteria garden. Beyond that was a bed of flowers made of light. And today, there was the added gift of falling snow. The illumination caught the snowflakes, giving the entire garden an unearthly splendor.

It was like a dream come true.

There were couples all around him. Groups of college kids. A few families. Sakuta was the only person here alone.

No matter where he looked, all he found was night skies, snow, and lights. No signs of Shouko. It was slowly dawning on him that he'd come all this way to confirm that obvious truth with his own eyes.

Big Shouko no longer existed.

Her future would never come.

It had been lost forever.

Taken away…by Sakuta's hand.

"……"

He was past feeling anything.

He wasn't cold. He wasn't sad.

He knew this sight was beautiful, but it didn't move him at all.

To no one in particular, he whispered, "Gotta get home," as if he'd just remembered something important.

He didn't really remember how he got home.

Had he walked the whole way? Taken a train? Maybe a bus? The memories were fuzzy. But he made it there. As his apartment building came into sight, he saw someone standing by the side of the road.

A tall girl with an umbrella. She looked cold and was rubbing her hands together around the umbrella handle. She must have been standing there a long time. There was a lot of snow piled up on that giant umbrella.

"…Mai," Sakuta said, stopping in his tracks.

Mai saw him, too. Their eyes met. Her eyes glistened with relief. Then she bit her lip, stopping herself before she started crying.

That was all she did.

She didn't call his name and she didn't run to him.

She just held his gaze and waited for him to come to her.

"…Oh. That's why."

They'd each made a promise. He'd come home and she'd be there

waiting for him. She'd stuck to her word and had been patiently waiting for him to keep his.

"......!"

His tear ducts had completely lost it by now. All the crying he'd
done, and they were still making more. Warm tears streamed down
his cheeks.

He didn't try to wipe them. Pelted with snow, Sakuta took one step
after another, back to Mai. Each step brought him closer home.

Remembering everything that had brought him here…

Reflecting on the meaning of each step…

Sakuta's feet took him the rest of the way.

Then he was under Mai's umbrella. This was the only spot with
almost no snow.

"……"

Mai said nothing. She wordlessly handed him the umbrella.

"……"

There was an expectant look in her eyes.

He knew what she was waiting for. Any kid would. It was what
everyone said after coming back.

"I'm home, Mai," he said.

She slowly smiled.

"Welcome back, Sakuta."

Her voice was warm and welcoming.

Chapter
3

NO Dreams of
HIS First Love

1

He could smell bread toasting.

There was a sizzle from the stove. Eggs were frying.

Slippers went flapping past his head. Then he heard the curtains slide open, and light hit his eyelids.

The footsteps came back toward Sakuta.

He felt something close in on him, and then something slapped his forehead.

"It's past ten! Wake up!"

"I'm already up, Mai," he said, not opening his eyes.

"Then eat before it gets cold. I've gotta go."

She moved away. Wanting to give chase, Sakuta tried to open his eyes only to find them stuck together. He'd cried a lot the day before and had fallen asleep crying. The tears had dried, gluing his lashes together.

He rubbed his eyes and blinked a bunch before finally crawling out from under the living room *kotatsu*.

"Go where?" he asked, but he figured it out before the answer came.

One look at Mai told him. She was in uniform. Minegahara High's. She was putting a coat on over her blazer.

"School," she said.

"Winter vacation starts today," he said.

It better, or they were already super late. Guaranteed tardy.

"I didn't get my report card yet. I was out yesterday for the shoot."

"Then I'll come with," he said…and let out a huge yawn.

*   *   *

Sakuta ate the breakfast Mai made and quickly changed into his uniform. The two of them left the house together.

On the way to Fujisawa Station, Mai tried to hand comb his hair, but the bed head was stubborn and refused to yield.

Neither had proposed it aloud, but from the apartment to the station, they kept their hands clasped together.

They must have looked like a couple of lovesick kids.

They were being so open about it, the people they passed didn't even register her as *the* Mai Sakurajima.

The roads to Fujisawa Station had been plowed since the snow stopped, and there were a number of three-foot-tall snow mountains dotting the side of the road or sidewalks.

Both foot and car traffic were flowing smoothly. Just like any other day. The only areas left with snow were alleys where people seldom trod. One step off the main paths, and you were in four inches of unblemished snow.

But looking at those white expanses reminded him of the day before.

He would likely remember it every time it snowed. How Shouko had melted away before the snow did.

"……"

While he stared at the snow, something cold suddenly pressed against his cheek.

"Eep!" he yelped.

He spun around and found Mai holding a snowball in one hand, grinning.

"Wanna make a snowman later?" she asked.

"You're such a child, Mai."

"Oh? Then I'll do it alone."

"Wanna make one in the schoolyard?"

If the whole place was blanketed, they could make one impressive snowman.

"See, you *do* want to."

He didn't think Mai actually wanted to make a snowman. That wasn't the point. They were both trying to act normal, and even though it wasn't quite working…it was well worth the effort.

The words they exchanged didn't hold any real significance. But there was meaning in sharing meaningless words with each other. It was enough that they both understood. Knowing that would help them go on with their lives.

Fujisawa Station looked just like it always did. Crowded even at this hour. The only real change was that most students were on winter break, so even on a weekday, it felt more like a weekend.

Otherwise, it was exactly as bustling as you'd expect December 25 to be, but that alone was not extraordinary. It was just a normal Christmassy Christmas.

Yesterday had been an earth-shattering crisis.

And Sakuta was still feeling the aftershocks. The waters in his heart were still churning. The roar of the surf, the waves crashing in. And that was taking its toll physically; he'd spent all morning feeling like he was coming down with something. He had been trapped on the verge of panic and trying to act like everything was normal.

But the town was fine in every way that Sakuta's inner self wasn't.

Whatever happened to him, whatever he tried to do—it didn't affect the world at all.

Everyone else just went about their lives.

There were stands outside the department stores. Santas and reindeer were offering passersby cakes for half price. When Sakuta and Mai reached the platform, the train came in on time.

Sakuta had shed a lifetime's worth of tears, but sobbing wouldn't change the world. That was how it was. That was how the world was made.

He didn't resent it.

It felt like how things should be.

Sakuta himself would have walked right past a stranger on any number of occasions in the past, never noticing problems that weren't his own. Knowing, being involved, and being affected had given him a different perspective on things. He was invested in ways he had never been before.

And everyone went through life grappling with things like that.

"Beautiful," Mai murmured. She was gazing out the train windows.

"You are," he said.

"I meant the ocean."

That was a spine-chilling glare.

"Well, sure. Lovely."

"Me, or…?"

"The ocean."

"Hmph."

"You're super lovely, too."

"Whatever you say."

"I meant that, though…"

He was looking at her, but she wasn't looking at him. He gave up and peered out at the ocean, too.

Under the winter sky, the water caught the sunlight, glittering.

He saw this all the time. It was just the view from his regular commute. A daily routine. But today the ocean looked different.

It was prettier than usual.

And he felt that was because he'd chosen to live.

And because Mai was with him.

He'd taken this sight for granted, but in that moment, it was new again.

Something he saw every day might one day not be there. And that knowledge changed the way he saw things.

The train chugged on down the coast. Today the Enoden's notorious sluggishness felt good. It gave him time to soak in the view. Perfect for a wounded heart.

The brakes whined, and the train stopped.

Shichirigahama Station, Sakuta and Mai's destination.

Sakuta stood up and pulled Mai's hand, leading her out onto the platform.

"Isn't that Mai Sakurajima?"

Voices from the train behind them.

"You're kidding? In the flesh?"

"Is that her boyfriend?"

"He seems kinda...ordinary?"

He was pretty sure this was coming from the group of high school girls clustered around the door. He didn't bother to look back. They kept chattering, but the doors closed, and he couldn't hear the rest. The train pulled away, and their inquisitive looks were carried off toward Kamakura.

"Anyone who thinks you're ordinary is not a good judge of anything."

Not letting go of his hand, Mai ran her IC commuter pass through the gate. She seemed thoroughly pleased.

"But as an excellent judge of everything, Mai, what is your take?"

"......Hmm."

She gave him a sideways glance, observing him carefully.

"Okay, your face is on the ordinary side," she admitted. Blunt. Then she quickly added, "I like that I'm the only one who knows how cool you are."

Maybe this embarrassed her. She was suddenly walking very quickly. Since they were still holding hands, he wound up getting dragged along behind her.

"Mai."

"What?"

"Say that again."

"Nope. It'll just go to your head."

"Aw."

"This side of you isn't cool at all."

Mai glanced over her shoulder, smiling triumphantly. Clearly reveling in his look of dismay. She seemed happy. And that made Sakuta happy. Accumulating moments like this would make both their lives happy ones.

They weren't looking for anything out of the ordinary. Just moments that made them both smile in the midst of an ordinary day. Those were what made it all worthwhile.

This seemed like an obtainable goal—which was a load off his mind.

They crossed the tracks and slipped through the half-open gate onto the school grounds.

The path to the school building had been shoveled. One of the sports team had probably been roped into helping out. But the shoveling had given way to a snowball fight. There were the remains of missed throws all around.

They went in through the front doors.

"You find somewhere to kill time," Mai said, letting go of his hand. She was headed upstairs to the faculty office.

"I'll come with."

"I'm not parading my boyfriend around in front of the teachers."

"I don't wanna leave you!"

"It won't take long. Just wait."

She didn't let him get in another word.

"Kill time how?" he muttered, scratching his bed head.

He could think of only one option.

"But she won't be here *today*."

He headed toward the science lab anyway.

The door moved when he touched it—it wasn't locked.

The lights weren't on, but he called out "Futaba?" as he opened the door.

It was winter vacation, but Rio was standing at the chalkboard anyway. In her white lab coat, by the experiment table.

"……"

She took one look at him and froze, test tube in hand.

"You look like you've seen a ghost," he said, closing the door behind him.

Unlike the hall, the lab was quite warm and comfy thanks to the space heater doing a respectable job. it was quite cozy.

Warm as the room was, the view through the windows was all white. The sun reflected off the snow, brightening the room.

Rio's lips parted slightly, and a feeble voice leaked out. "Azusagawa…"

Before he could respond, her knees crumpled, and she hit the floor behind the table. Definitely less "sit" and more "collapse."

"Y-yo," he said, rushing over to her. "Futaba, you okay?"

He knelt down next to her and took the test tube away. It was empty, but he didn't want that breaking. He placed it safely in the rack on the table.

"…I'm not," he heard Rio whisper, but her voice caught in her throat, and he couldn't quite make it out.

"Futaba?" he said, peering into her face.

"I'm not okay!" Her head snapped up.

There were already huge drops falling from her eyes, which meant there was only one thing he could say.

"Sorry. I had you worried, huh?"

"I'm not okay…!" she said again. She had her hands balled up in fists, and she brought them down on Sakuta's knees. It didn't hurt at all. But her limp protest sure did make him feel powerfully guilty. He could feel a familiar tightness in his chest.

But that was nothing compared with how scared she must've been.

"I'm really sorry," he said. Not sure what else he could do.

"I'm not okay at all…" Rio delivered a whole flurry of feeble blows. "I thought I'd never see you again. I knew… I was sure you'd sacrifice yourself!"

"Yeah…"

She wasn't wrong. He'd made that choice once. But it hadn't worked out that way. He hadn't died. Because Mai had saved him. And she'd died in his stead.

To change that disastrous result, he'd come back from the future… and wound up here.

"But nobody called yesterday… Nobody told me you'd been in an accident. There was no coverage of it online or on the news…so I

thought maybe, just maybe, and waited all night. Except you didn't call to tell me you were okay!"

She didn't even try to hide her face or wipe away her tears. She just let all her feelings fly. Not at all how Rio usually handled things. There wasn't a trace of her usual logical calm. She wore everything on her sleeve as the words poured out.

And seeing her like this made Sakuta feel...warm. Going by what she was saying, it was safe to assume that Futaba was furious. They were fiery accusations. But the fists pounding away at him weren't trying to hurt him at all.

"Thank goodness," she said as her anger gave way to relief. The tears were still flowing. Her lab coat was getting very wet. "I'm glad you're alive, Azusagawa."

Rio finally managed a smile.

"Here," he said, grabbing a box of tissues from the table and handing it to her.

Rio took her glasses off. She must have recovered enough to feel shame again, because she snapped, "Don't look at me," and started wiping the tears.

She spent a few moments recovering and drying her glasses. Then she put them back on and turned toward Sakuta, eyes and nose still pretty red.

"What happened yesterday?"

"A lot," he said. "I dunno where to begin."

"How about this?" she said, pointing at the message scrawled across the complicated formula and graphs.

Look at me, Futaba!

The only words in his handwriting. The message he'd written trying to get her attention.

"That was you, right?"

"Yeah."

"And this?"

She showed him her phone. A short message to "Sakurajima-senpai" saved in the drafts folder.

This is Sakuta.

"So…yesterday…"

He tried to explain but suddenly couldn't breathe. Thoughts of big Shouko suddenly filled his mind, and his voice broke. He felt ready to cry. He managed to avoid breaking down by taking a very deep breath.

"Yesterday, I did what I had to do."

He was mostly telling himself that.

He stood up, and when Rio looked at him, he took her hands and pulled her to her feet. She seemed steady enough, but it felt like she'd collapse again if he let go, so he led her to a chair.

Then he started talking, as if reviewing his own actions.

He told her about how he'd gone ahead into the future.

About his Adolescence Syndrome.

How his own weakness had given him a second shot.

And about the choice he'd made.

He told her everything—including what that choice meant.

There was no beating around the bush. Just plain truth.

Rio listened in silence. The only reactions she offered were a few shifts in her breathing or little nods of encouragement to keep him going.

When he finished, she still said nothing.

Instead, she filled a beaker with water, placed it on the wire mesh, and lit the alcohol lamp. They waited for it to boil, and then she made instant coffee for both of them.

Her coffee was in a proper mug, but Sakuta's was, as always, in the same beaker she'd used to boil the water. The coffee was on the strong side. Both of them took a sip.

He let the bitter liquid rest on his tongue. Felt it at the back of his nose. Then he appreciated the warmth of it sliding down his throat.

Finally, Rio spoke.

"So a lot happened," she said.

Neither approving nor disapproving. Neither encouraging nor comforting. Just an acknowledgment of understanding. And for that, he was eternally grateful.

They finished their bitter coffee in silence.

Neither one of them could find the words. He'd already told Rio everything. There was nothing left for him to say.

So when his beaker was empty, Sakuta stood up.

"Azusagawa."

"Mm?"

"I'm glad you're alive."

"……"

"I mean that."

"…Mm."

He didn't have a proper response. Emotions were swirling inside him, and he wanted to say something to acknowledge her words and feelings. But if he tried, he knew he'd start crying, so he said nothing instead.

"That's all," Rio said, and she turned toward the windows. Then she blinked. "Is that Sakurajima?"

She jumped up and moved over to the window. She reached for the lock and opened it.

A blast of cold air rushed in.

Sakuta came up next to her, looking out in the yard.

A blanket of white snow covered everything.

It hadn't snowed at all last year, so this was their first time seeing Minegahara High like this.

The snow must have forced the baseball and soccer teams to cancel practice. There was only one person out there.

And that was Mai.

She was carefully picking her way across the untouched field of snow. It looked pretty slippery, and she almost lost her balance a few times—there was definitely some arm flailing involved—but she made it to the center of the yard, looking delighted.

Then she knelt down and put her hands on the snow.

"Sakurajima, what are you doing?" Rio called.

Meanwhile, Sakuta had his foot on the windowsill.

"Alley-oop," he said, and he jumped out.

"Azusagawa?"

"We're gonna make a snowman."

"Huh?" Rio gaped at him.

"Wanna come?"

Rio looked from Sakuta to Mai. Then she smiled, as if she'd figured it out.

"Too cold for me," she said before she closed the window.

She said something through the glass, but he couldn't make it out.

But he could tell from her expression.

She didn't want to be a third wheel.

2

Sakuta and Mai took their time and ended up with three snowmen. Two of them were maybe thirty inches tall, the result of a competition between them. The biggest of them was as tall as Sakuta, and that had required the two of them to work together, rolling massive snowballs around.

But at this size, the two of them had been unable to get the head up on the body, so in the end they convinced Rio to come out and help. The head alone was a good thirty inches across, and even with three of them, it had been too heavy, so when Yuuma's team took a break, they'd grabbed him, and the four of them had finished the snowman together.

It was entirely frivolous. They could just as easily have quit while they were ahead. But standing before this giant snowman gave them a real sense of accomplishment.

They placed the snowmen next to the entrance, like they were watching over the students as they came in.

Mai took a picture on her phone, looking thoroughly satisfied.

On the train back, Mai flipped through the photos she'd taken and happily showed them to Sakuta.

The two of them with the snowmen. A bunch of shots with Rio and Yuuma, too. Nothing remarkable, just a bunch of fun photos.

"It's very 'high school,'" Mai said. She *was* in high school, so this should have seemed odd, but it made perfect sense to Sakuta.

"Totally," he said.

It fit the stereotype exactly. It was like one of those happy memories from a flashback on a TV show about teenage drama. It slotted right into that formula.

They were still going through the photos when the train reached Fujisawa Station.

They went out the gates and across the bridge toward the JR building. But halfway there, Sakuta stopped.

Mai noticed a moment later and turned back.

"Sakuta?"

"That dog…," he said.

He was looking at a large dog lying at the end of the passage. A Labrador retriever.

There were two women with it—one in her forties and one in her twenties—wearing light-green staff jackets, collecting money to train Seeing Eye dogs.

He'd seen people fundraising here any number of times before. He'd even seen this exact Labrador lying there before.

But this was the first time he'd ever stopped.

He took out his wallet and emptied the change onto his palm. Maybe two hundred yen total.

Carrying it, he went over to the older woman and said, "Here."

"Thanks for your help!" she said, holding out the box. He dropped the change in. "Wow, big spender!" she said with a smile.

"It's less than it sounded like," he said.

"We're grateful for any support you can offer."

The woman clearly meant that. There were a slew of people streaming past behind him.

"He's happy, too, see?" she said, pointing down at the Lab. It was wagging its tail. Those eyes peering up at Sakuta were so pure it made him feel guilty.

He didn't think it was benevolence that had driven him to donate. Sakuta knew better than that.

He'd chosen a life with Mai over Shouko's future.

And it was the lingering residue of that choice that motivated him.

Like doing something good would earn him forgiveness.

Like doing something good would lead to little Shouko's recovery.

What he could offer was hardly a fair exchange, but this amounted to a prayer to whatever gods might be watching.

Next to him, Mai dropped in a few coins, too.

"Er, wait, are you...?"

The twentysomething girl recognized Mai Sakurajima and held out her hand. Mai shook it.

"Are we allowed to pet the dog?"

"Yes. He's being a good boy, so please let him know."

Mai patted the Lab on the head. It closed its eyes, looking happy.

"Hey, is that...?"

The crowd around them was starting to notice the celebrity in their midst, so Sakuta and Mai quickly left the Seeing Eye dog behind. They crossed the JR station and went out the other side. They were quickly lost in the throng of people.

"Nothing's ever simple," Mai murmured, staring straight ahead.

He wasn't sure she'd meant for him to hear. It felt kind of like she was just talking to herself.

"I agree," he said. He was well aware she hadn't been looking for an answer. But he was sure they felt the same way.

There were people out there in need of help. People they didn't know and had never met. That had made it easy to forget. They might see suffering out of the corner of their eyes but that was all too simple to ignore as somebody else's problems.

But knowing how little Shouko was forced to wait for a donor heart meant they were *involved*. It would *always* matter to them. Meeting

Shouko had taught Sakuta that maybe it would be his future self who ended up saving those in need.

Like Mai said, things could never be simple again. Knowing how Shouko's condition made her suffer had opened their eyes. They were glad to have made this discovery, but given the implications for Shouko…it was impossible to be happy without reservation.

But some realizations only came like this.

If they were easy, fewer people would have hurried past that Labrador without a second thought.

And maybe the circle of organ donors would be a lot bigger. Little Shouko might have had her operation ages ago and already be healthy.

But that wasn't how the world worked.

Too many things were lost without anyone realizing, without anyone getting the chance to notice, without anyone knowing. Nobody even realized this was happening.

Nobody was to blame for it. It wasn't anybody's fault. People just weren't made that way. Sakuta himself had been clueless until he was personally involved.

Everyone had things they had to do or wanted to do. And they were busy giving it their all, or were already doing everything they could, or were too engrossed to pay attention to anything else.

They might have homework or real work that had to be done by tomorrow. They might have videos they had to catch up on so they could talk to their friends. They might have texts they had to respond to. Shopping that had to be done before dinner. Rooms to be cleaned before their parents yelled at them.

All of these were trivial compared with someone's life. But to the people concerned, the scale of the problem didn't matter; these were still things that couldn't just be ignored. And it was human nature to focus on the problem at hand.

If everyone were focused on the problems of others, that would actually be kinda creepy. Seven billion people worried about all seven billion other people would be exhausting. No one would ever be able to keep up with so many worries.

All Sakuta could do was what he wanted to do and what he felt he should do.

No grandiose expectations and no wallowing in futility.

If he kept that in mind, he could manage.

And this moment settled everything.

"Uh, Mai…," he said, stopping in his tracks.

"Hmm?"

"I wanna make a stop before we head home."

"Going to see Shouko? I'll come, too."

She started walking toward the hospital. Sakuta quickly caught up, and Mai took his hand.

He knocked on the door of room 301, but there was no answer.

"…Coming in," he said, and he slid the door open.

The room was dark and quiet. The sound of silence. The low hum of the minifridge, the rushing of blood in his ears, the sound of his own steps, the rustling of his clothes, and the sound of his own breath.

The lights were out, and the curtains drawn. Guarded by silence, the air in the room felt stagnant and old. Like this hospital room had been left behind in the distant past.

He looked to the bed, but Shouko wasn't there. She was in the ICU. Without special permission, only her family could visit.

On the empty bed stood three beautifully wrapped presents and a teddy bear with a big bow. Christmas presents from her parents and the hospital staff.

"I totally forgot," he said.

Yesterday, he hadn't thought he'd live to see December 25. Until he experienced Mai's death, he'd assumed today would never come. It had never occurred to him to get her a present. That had been way beyond his capabilities.

"I hope Shouko gets better," Mai said, setting the teddy bear upright.

"Yeah."

If she got better and was released, she could bring Hayate over to play. They'd wash the two cats together, get shampoo all over them, and laugh themselves silly.

Maybe he had no right to think like this, not after destroying her chance at a future. He felt like he didn't deserve to wish for her recovery.

But he couldn't stop himself.

No matter what anyone said otherwise.

From the bottom of his heart, he hoped—prayed—that Shouko would get better.

Sakuta had even poured that prayer into the snowman they made.

Please save Makinohara.

Those feelings, too, were genuine. If there was a way for her to survive, he wanted that more than anything. Sakuta had been given a chance to save her. But that had proved to be the one choice he couldn't take. Doing so would mean he couldn't make Mai happy.

Mai, meanwhile, had found something on the side table and picked it up.

"Whatcha looking at?"

"This."

She held out a piece of paper. A printout from school, browned with age. He'd seen this before—Shouko's schedule for the future.

She'd been given this as an assignment in the fourth grade. But knowing full well her condition didn't leave her with much of a future, she'd been unable to bring herself to fill it out completely.

The doctors had told her that without a heart transplant, she was unlikely to graduate junior high. So how could she make plans beyond that?

Shouko couldn't imagine herself in high school and college or all grown up.

Sakuta scanned the schedule, reading what she'd written there.

"……?"

He immediately noticed the irregularity.

It had changed.

He remembered there being a lot more here.

The penciled writing ended in the middle of junior high. Before she even graduated.

The last time he'd seen it, it was filled out all the way to college. That was why Shouko had wanted his opinion—because she didn't remember writing the later entries.

And this wasn't just a lapse of memory. The first time she showed him the schedule, it was filled out through high school. But when he looked again a few days later, he'd seen the college section filled out, too.

And there were traces of that on the page in his hand.

It looked like she'd written all the way to college and then erased it. He could still see faint traces of the letters.

> *Graduate junior high.*
>
> *Enter a high school with a view of the sea! (Minegahara High is my first choice!)*
>
> *Meet the boy I'm destined to be with.*
>
> *Graduate in good health!*
>
> *Start college.*
>
> *Reunite with the boy of destiny.*
>
> *Tell him how I feel!*

He could make out just enough of the entries to tell they were what he'd remembered.

But he didn't know why they'd been erased.

Or what was happening.

Looking at this just reminded him of how Shouko's actual future had been erased, which hurt. He remembered how she'd struggled to smile. How she'd smiled anyway, not wanting to worry her parents or Sakuta. Struggling against fears far bigger than her own body. Frustration got Sakuta's tear ducts going again. Any second now, they'd start pumping out the waterworks. But this was the future he'd chosen. He couldn't cry here. Not in front of Mai, and definitely not in Shouko's hospital room.

"I'm gonna go get us some drinks," he said.

He handed Mai the printout and left the room alone.

He moved down the empty hall, keeping his head high.

His eyes on the two rows of unadorned fluorescent lights.

Pointlessly counting them seemed to help stave off the tears. He took an elevator to the first floor—just to be extra sure, he'd picked the farthest possible vending machines.

By the time he reached the row of them by the gift shop, he was in better shape.

He took a thousand-yen note out of his wallet and fed it into the slot.

He first pressed the button for warm milk tea. That was for Mai.

Then he bought a blue-labeled sports drink for himself. The sixteen-ounce bottle fell with a thunk.

Would Mai praise him for remembering to buy something for her? Would she laugh because he'd picked the one she did commercials for? Imagining how she might react, he bent down to grab the drinks.

And something wet dripped onto his hand.

"Huh?"

Caught off guard, he made a weird noise. He looked down at his hand, doing a double and triple take. His hand was definitely coated in clear fluid.

A moment later, he realized this was relief. All he was doing was buying one drink for Mai and another that she advertised, then imagining how she might react when he brought them back—and the tiny joy of this everyday action had left him in tears.

Shedding tears over something totally commonplace. A slow, gentle warmth was wrapping its arms around him. There was no way to resist it. Nothing could stop tears of joy. He certainly couldn't. Why would he even want to?

Unable to grab the drinks, he leaned against the machine, curling up in a ball. His shoulders heaving. He didn't want to worry any strangers, so he stifled his voice…and waited for this gentle embrace to pass.

And as he did, he realized something.

Something very simple.

"I'm already happy."

If he could cry like this…

And that fact brought a new wave of tears.

"I'm…already happy," he whispered. It was for himself. He wanted to hear it out loud.

Mindful of the small happiness close at hand.

Mindful of the happiness he already had.

Reminding himself that this was what happiness really was.

He'd taken quite a detour, so when Sakuta got back to room 301, a good half hour had passed.

He was carrying the milk tea and the sports drink, as well as a snowman small enough to hold in one hand.

"This one's for you, Mai."

He handed her the tea. It wasn't exactly warm anymore, but Mai didn't mention that or how long he'd been away.

Instead, she looked at the snowman. "Christmas present for Shouko?" she asked.

One glance at his eyes would make it obvious he'd been crying, but she pretended not to notice.

He put the snowman in the empty freezer of the minifridge. Then he grabbed a sticky note and wrote *Snowman Storage* on it. The last thing he wanted was for the nurses or Shouko's mom opening it unawares and freaking out.

Mai took a swig of her tea, and he undid the cap on his own drink.

The snap of it was oddly satisfying. He'd lost a lot of fluids crying, so he chugged half the bottle in one go.

"You look like you want a reward," Mai said, raising an eyebrow.

"Just stay with me forever."

"Is that all?"

Judging from her smile, she'd really liked that answer.

3

As they stepped out of the hospital, Mai said, "Oof, I completely forget there's absolutely nothing in the fridge."

So they stopped at a grocery store on the way home.

They bought food for the next few days. Sakuta took the big bag, and Mai the little one, and they kept their free hands clasped together the rest of the way home.

Outside their buildings, Mai didn't pull away. She followed Sakuta onto the elevator in his building. It was obvious she was planning on spending the evening at his place. Since this was entirely a good thing, he elected not to mention it.

At this rate, odds were high she'd cook for him.

Looking forward to that, he opened the door. He immediately had second thoughts about bringing Mai with him.

There were shoes lined up in the entrance—and he didn't recognize all of them. The first pair were Kaede's—she'd clearly kicked them off the second she got back and left them fall where they may. But the second pair were neatly lined up, heel to heel.

"Oh, you're back!"

He heard socks sliding along the wood floor.

His sister, Kaede, had come running out to meet him. It was still weird seeing her hair cropped to shoulder-length. It had only been a few days since their trip to the hair salon. And Kaede had spent most of that at their grandparents' house, so Sakuta hadn't really had time to get used to her new look.

"Oh, Mai! Welcome home."

"Thanks for having me," Mai said, tearing her eyes off the extra pair of shoes.

Kaede was definitely not the only one here. And there wasn't much doubt about who the other person might be. It was obviously Sakuta's father, having driven Kaede home.

For a second, Sakuta debated whether to stop Mai from taking her shoes off.

But since they were already here, he decided it was best to own it. And since they didn't live with their father anymore, maybe this was a good chance to formally introduce Mai to him. No need to give anyone more reasons to worry, and no reason to keep putting it off.

It was just a little embarrassing. That was the only real problem.

"Dad! Sakuta's home," Kaede said, calling down the hall.

His father poked his head out of the living room.

"Welcome back, Sakuta," he said quietly.

"Thanks, Dad."

Not about to lose this fight, Sakuta kept his tone every bit as subdued. He saw Mai bob her head out of the corner of his eye. His father did the same.

"So, uh, Mai...this is my dad," Sakuta said. "And this is my girlfriend, Mai Sakurajima."

He wasn't sure how else to put it, so he just decided to go for the direct approach.

This wasn't their first time meeting. They'd bumped into each other at the hospital during the trouble with Kaede, so they were at least aware of each other. His father was past the point of being surprised by the arrival of a famous actress.

"Thanks for taking care of my son."

"Please forgive the delayed introduction—and sorry to spring it on you like this."

"No, I know you're busy."

"Even so..."

"......"

"……"

Running out of formalities, they settled into an awkward silence.

"I'm not used to these things," his father said, smiling awkwardly.

"Get it together, Dad." Kaede elbowed him in the ribs.

"I know, but it's unreal enough having the girl from the TV in front of me, and then when you say she's Sakuta's… I don't know what to say."

"You're totally embarrassing me."

"Kaede, you freaked out, too."

"I know, but…"

"Sakuta," Mai said, poking him in the back. "I'm gonna head on home."

"No, I was just leaving," their dad said. He did have his briefcase in hand. "Can't leave your mother on her own for long."

That comment was for Sakuta. But he knew Mai understood. He'd explained the situation a long time ago—how Kaede had been bullied, how she developed Adolescence Syndrome, and how their mother had lost confidence in her parenting abilities and had a nervous breakdown.

Sakuta put his shoes back on.

"I'll walk you down," he said.

"No, you're fine."

Sakuta ignored his father's protests and stepped out the door first. Mai followed. Kaede waved good-bye at the door, and they left her to guard the fort. The three of them took the elevator down.

It made no stops on the way, and they headed right back out the front doors and paused in the street outside.

Sakuta's father looked at him and then turned to Mai.

"We don't live together, so I may not be able to speak with much authority. But I know Sakuta agreed to live like this for his mother's and Kaede's sake. I believe that's indicative of a considerate soul."

Blindsided by this speech, Sakuta was immediately deeply uncomfortable. He did *not* want Mai hearing any of this and desperately wanted to interrupt. But his father was clearly speaking from the heart so he didn't dare say a word.

"I'm also acutely conscious of the burden I've placed on him. Perhaps I don't have the right to ask, but I hope you'll stay by his side."

"Happily," Mai said softly. "I'm the one who wants to be here."

His father looked relieved. He smiled faintly. Sakuta had never seen his father smile like that. He was taken aback but also relieved. Mai had helped reassure him.

"Take care," Sakuta said.

"Come see your mother after New Year's," his father said and turned to walk away. He must have been parked in the lot toward the station.

He was soon out of sight.

Mai sighed in relief. "That was nerve-racking," she said.

"Even you get fazed sometimes, huh?"

"What do you think I am?"

"My bride-to-be?"

"Well, that's not gonna happen if your father hates my guts," she said, matching his jokey tone. "Some people just have it in for celebrities."

"It doesn't seem like that's gonna be a problem."

"Well, he is *your* dad."

He wasn't sure how that was relevant, but talking about his family was always awkward, so he elected to change the subject.

"I guess I'll have to meet your parents one of these days."

"Pfft, hardly."

Mai rejected the idea outright and headed back inside. Realizing she couldn't get in without a key, she pulled the spare out of her pocket. She still had the key he'd given her yesterday.

He quickly followed, and they got on the elevator together.

The rift with her parents—especially her mother—was bad enough that she didn't even want to discuss them.

"I dunno if I should tell you this...," Sakuta began with some hesitation.

"......"

Mai kept her eyes on the floor number.

"But after the accident…in the other future."

He could feel his heart starting to race, but he forced himself to keep speaking.

"At the hospital, your mother came running. She was desperate. Pleading with the doctors to save you."

"……"

Mai said nothing.

"She also slapped me really hard and demanded I bring you back."

"I know she still cares."

"……"

"But I don't want to hear whatever opinions she might have about you. So not…not now."

"Okay."

The elevator dinged.

He opened the front door, and they stepped in. Kaede came padding back out with Nasuno in her arms. She seemed like she'd been waiting for them for a reason.

"Sakuta," she said, looking tense.

"What?"

"Do you have a minute?"

"I'm busy flirting."

"Eww."

"Nothing matters more than— Ow!"

Mai had rapped the back of his head. In lieu of further scolding, she said, "I'll just borrow your sink," and headed farther in.

"So? What?" Sakuta said, meeting Kaede's eye.

"I have a favor to ask."

"More allowance?"

"No."

"Whew."

"I mean, also that, but…"

"Oh? Our finances are in crisis."

"I want you to help me practice," she said, scowling.

"Oh, that? Sure."

"Do you actually get it?" She looked dubious.

"School, right?"

"Y-yeah," she said, somewhat taken aback. Did she really think he wouldn't understand?

"You're starting there third term, yeah?"

"Mm."

She nodded.

He felt like this was a promise she'd made to the other Kaede.

"So tomorrow…"

"Have your uniform ready."

"I already did *that*."

She glared at him, as if resenting being treated like a kid. But if she didn't want that, she should probably stop making sulky faces.

"Tomorrow, then."

"Mm!"

Kaede nodded emphatically and headed back to the living room. She still seemed a bit tense, but Sakuta thought making this promise was a real accomplishment.

When today was over, it would be tomorrow.

And once it was tomorrow, they could do tomorrow things.

Taking it one day at time, as the future drew near.

Whatever tomorrow held, they had to go to it. Sakuta had chosen a future that had a tomorrow in it. He would live the life big Shouko had given him.

4

As promised, the next day Sakuta helped Kaede practice going to school. They started with her putting her uniform on and doing a lap of their apartment building. On the second day, they headed toward Kaede's junior high.

Since it was winter vacation, there was no one else wearing that uniform, and Kaede was concerned that this drew more attention, but each day, they made it closer to her school.

By day three, they got close enough to see the green net around the school grounds. They ran into some students heading in for practice, so they beat a hasty retreat, but they were making progress much faster than Sakuta had anticipated.

He felt her goal of attending school once vacation ended was obtainable.

In the afternoon of December 29, Sakuta took Kaede on a train to Ueno, figuring it would be a good break from her training.

"I'm in junior high now! Going to the zoo with your brother is just mortifying."

Kaede grumbled the whole way, but once she actually got there...

"Sakuta! It's a panda! Look at the panda! It's eating bamboo!"

She was more excited than the literal children there with their parents.

In the gift shop on the way out, she even begged for a stuffed animal.

"Sakuta, this one's really cute!"

"That's nice."

"Really cute!"

"You've got one at home."

"But it's so cute!"

"Isn't third year a bit old for stuffed animals?"

"I'm still first year inside!"

As a result, Sakuta's already empty wallet wound up even emptier. He owed Tomoe money as it was, so he really couldn't afford to splurge any more.

In an attempt to make up for that—well, not just for that—Sakuta took as many shifts as he could at work.

Some of those days were specially requested by his manager, on the grounds that it was hard to staff shifts that time of year. But Sakuta didn't refuse any. He didn't have anything else planned, and there were times when staying busy helped.

On the thirtieth, he and Tomoe were both working—the first time they'd seen each other since he came back from the future on December 24.

On break, he returned her watch and the three thousand yen.

"Everything's okay now?" she asked.

"That three thousand yen is all I have, so it's going to be a very frugal New Year's."

"Not that. I mean…which one are you?"

"Both. We fused."

"……"

"That's why I'm okay. No need to stay worried, I promise."

"Well, if you're fine, then…fine."

She sure didn't look fine. She had her lips pursed, evidently not entirely satisfied with his explanation.

"Then stop making that face already."

"I just wanted to help you, you know."

That was an awfully cute thing to say.

"You may not realize it, but you were the MVP this time."

He meant that.

If it weren't for Tomoe, his trip through time would have gotten him nowhere. He'd have been forced to gnaw his fingers off, watching the worst unfold again. Like hell on earth. Just the thought of that was enough to make him break out in a cold sweat.

"I owe you big-time."

"I didn't do anything."

"By way of thanks, use that three thousand yen and order any parfait you like."

"Oh, uh, sure…but wait, this is *my* three thousand yen!"

"Don't sweat the details."

"Three thousand yen is not a detail!"

"……"

"D-don't just go quiet on me."

"This job's a lot more fun when you're around, Koga."

Being able to goof around with her was a relief, and it caused something sincere to slip out. Looking at her, he felt like he was one step away from tearing up again.

"Senpai, are you sure you're okay?"

She leaned in, worried.

"Maybe not… Augh, my guts are rumbling. Man the floor for me!"

He quickly retreated to the bathroom.

When he got home from work, it was time to eat Mai's dinner. She was now cooking every night.

It was usually just Sakuta, Mai, and Kaede, but today Nodoka had tagged along. Her sister complex was in overdrive, and she'd stuck to Mai's side like glue the whole time she was cooking.

Sakuta asked why.

"She had a bad dream this morning," Mai said.

"What about?"

"Don't wanna talk about it," Nodoka snapped.

It didn't seem like he was gonna pry anything out of her. Peeling an onion, he glanced Mai's way.

"She dreamed I was hit by a car."

"……"

Given that Sakuta had personally lived through that once, it took him a minute to say anything. Even in a dream, it would be unspeakable. Nodoka loved Mai almost as much as he did.

"Well, fair enough. I'll let you borrow my Mai for today."

"I don't need your permission, and she's not yours to begin with."

She did cheer up eventually, and they ate together.

"You oughtta learn to cook, Toyohama. Instead of coming here."

"I'm here to make sure you don't try anything."

"Mai isn't your mom."

"She cooks for you on a daily basis! My sister ain't your mom, either!"

"No, she's my future wife."

"If you and Mai get married, would that make Nodoka your sister-inlaw?" Kaede asked as she chewed on a potato.

"……" Nodoka's chopsticks froze in midair.

"I don't need a go-go girl for a sister."

"Pfft, why are you talking like it's the sixties?!" Kaede laughed.

"……"

"What?" Nodoka glared.

"Maybe it wouldn't be so bad being your older brother."

"Drop dead."

"Don't say that. It's too sad."

Like Kaede, he was munching on Mai's meat and potatoes. He glanced toward Mai and found her eyes on him.

"I knew it!" Nodoka said, totally reading that wrong. "Something happened over Christmas!"

"Nothing like what you're thinking, Nodoka," Mai said serenely.

"I-I'm not thinking— Th-the food was great!"

She fled to the sink with her empty plate.

"In other words, it was a way bigger deal than what Toyohama had in mind."

"R-really?" Kaede gasped. "What did you do?"

"Don't exaggerate," Mai said, stomping his foot under the table.

And thus, they whiled away the evening.

And thus, Sakuta's life went on.

He savored each day, one at a time.

Trying to act natural.

Laughing at ordinary things, joking around, getting Mai to scold him, getting Rio to scoff at him, teasing Tomoe, playing dumb with Kaede, pissing Nodoka off, making Yuuma laugh…just as he always had.

And in the middle of all those normal everyday things, he'd be hit by a sudden urge to cry, and he'd cling to that until it passed. The smallest things could remind him of how lucky he was to be alive. And the more peaceful his days were, the worse his guilt became. His tears were a prayer to save little Shouko. Sakuta was tossing on the stormy seas of his heart.

If he tried to bottle them up, he'd stop functioning at all. He didn't have much choice besides staying perfectly still until the wave receded.

But he knew, in time, he'd move past this.

If he took one day at a time, the year would eventually draw to an end.

Maybe something would change next year.

Winter vacation would end, third term would begin, Kaede would be in school again…and January would be over before anyone knew it.

In February, Mai would give him some chocolate…and in March, she'd graduate from Minegahara.

Nothing Sakuta felt could stop the flow of time.

Regardless of his feelings, the seasons would turn, and spring would come.

There was nothing he could do about it.

And not long after he came to that realization…

…the phone rang.

December 31. New Year's Eve.

Sakuta was up at seven, ready to help Kaede practice going to school. He washed his face, ate breakfast, and was waiting for Kaede to finish changing into her uniform when the call came.

He moved over to the living room phone.

As he reached for the receiver, he froze.

"Sakuta?" Kaede asked. She'd stepped out of her room and saw the look on his face. He couldn't answer. His eyes were locked on the phone's screen. He recognized the number on it. It was Shouko's cell phone.

That meant one of two things.

Either it was good news.

Or it wasn't.

"……"

He slowly let all the air out of his lungs and then picked up the phone.

"This is Azusagawa."

"Oh…I'm sorry to call this early. This is Makinohara…"

A grown woman's voice.

"Makinohara's mother, right? It's me."

"Oh, good. I hate to spring this on you…"

Each word she said was making his heart beat out of his chest.

"No problem," he managed.

His throat spasmed like he was suffocating.

"I found your number…on Shouko's phone."

"Right."

All he could manage was the shortest of replies. The idea of asking what had happened hid itself at the back of his mouth. His tongue was afraid to even form the question. Every crack and crevice of his body was filled with trepidation.

Not knowing where to look, his eyes turned to the clock. It wasn't even eight thirty yet. Like Shouko's mom said, it was a bit early to call anyone. So if she was calling now, there must have been a reason.

"Will you come see Shouko?"

"……"

"Please."

Her voice shook. He couldn't stave off the question any longer.

"What happened?" he asked, feeling like he was pushing through a forest of thorns. His lips quivered. The hand holding the receiver shook. The cord rattled against the wall.

"She doesn't…" Two words, and Shouko's mother's voice broke. "Shouko doesn't have…"

Her voice was wet with tears. Her beloved daughter's name blotted out with grief.

Sakuta fought off the urge to clap his hands over his ears. The anguish in her mother's voice was making his whole body groan. His chest ached. It was like someone had reached out and wrapped their hand around his heart.

Anyone who knew Shouko's condition would immediately suspect bad news if he was calling this early. It was the natural assumption.

"I just got off the phone with her mother."

"Oh."

"She doesn't have long."

"You're headed there?"

"Yeah."

"I'll come, too."

"Okay."

"See you there," Rio said, ready to hang up.

"Futaba…," he said, stopping her.

He hadn't gotten to his real point yet. He'd called Rio before Mai because there was something he needed to ask.

"What?"

Her guard went up immediately.

And hearing that made him feel a little better. The tension in her voice proved that what he was about to say wasn't completely crazy.

"There is a way, right?"

"……"

He heard her gulp. The sound was so small he would have missed it if he hadn't been listening for it. She didn't say a word.

"A remote possibility, but one that might be worth the risk."

"……"

"We might still be able to save her."

His hand tightened around the receiver, clutching at it.

"……"

Rio still said nothing.

"Until Mai was safe, I couldn't think about anything else. So I forgot. But Makinohara's own Adolescence Syndrome is still going strong. Seeing her future schedule in her hospital room reminded me of that."

"……"

"Everything after junior high had been erased. I could still see the pencil marks where someone had rubbed them out."

But he kept the receiver on his ear because hearing this out wa only thing he could do.

"The doctor said...she doesn't... She doesn't have much...time I'm sorry."

Her mother's sobs proved how bad things were. They robbed Sak of the luxury of hesitation.

"Okay. I'll be right there."

He managed to get that out clearly.

"Thank you...and sorry..."

"See you at the hospital."

He put the receiver down slowly, not letting it make a sound. Doing all he could to dethorn the news her mother had delivered. To wrap it all up in cotton.

She was the one who loved Shouko the most. The one who'd prayed hardest for Shouko's recovery. And that meant there was no one more delicate than her now.

"Sakuta?" Kaede said, looking worried. He saw himself in her eyes and realized his cheeks were wet.

"Sorry, Kaede. Gotta head to the hospital. You okay skipping practice today?"

"Yeah, sure..."

She was clearly more worried about him.

He wiped his cheeks, trying to show he was fine. Then he picked up the phone again. He punched in a number from memory. He'd dialed it so many times he didn't even have to think.

He heard it ringing.

Once. Twice. It picked up halfway through the third ring.

"Azusagawa?" Rio said, sounding fully alert.

"You were awake already?"

"I always get up at seven."

It was very Rio to keep that schedule even on vacation.

"...Something happen with Shouko?" she asked before he could say a word.

There was nothing mechanical about that change. It had obviously been done by a human hand. By someone. Manually. He was sure of it.

"It was Makinohara who wrote and erased it. She most likely did both at the same time…in fourth grade."

"……"

Rio said nothing, but he could hear the restlessness in her breath. He could tell she kept almost saying something and deciding against it. It was probably her wondering whether she should push him away from the heart of the matter. But he was already too close to it for that to work.

"Three years ago, Makinohara wrote out her schedule and then erased it. Her fears of the future caused her Adolescence Syndrome. Am I right?"

"Do you get what you're saying, Azusagawa?" she finally asked him directly. But she knew the answer.

"I'm saying we aren't in the present. This is the future."

"……"

"So if we can save the 'present' Makinohara—the one in fourth grade—then we should also be able to save the junior high school one."

"Azusagawa."

Rio called his name, as if trying to get through to him.

"There's a chance, right?"

"That's not even worth calling a 'chance.'"

"……"

"What you're saying is *just* wishful thinking."

"Harsh."

"Not much better than hoping she finds a donor today."

"I'm sure you're right, but…"

"Shouko came from the future, and you went back four days—in both cases, that was possible because you were the ones with the Adolescence Syndrome. A single consciousness that divided into two, with differing perceptions of the flow of time. Shouko's in the ICU. Do you think she could save herself if she went back in time?"

"I think it would be hard even if she wasn't in the ICU."

Sakuta didn't think a thirteen-year-old in need of a heart transplant could save herself. Sakuta was a lot older, and he sure couldn't do it. Grown-ups couldn't, either. That was exactly why her parents had suffered so much.

"Shouko's condition isn't something a do-over would help. Going back three years won't lead to any revolutionary medical advancements. All she'll do is live three very similar years and come right back to this moment."

"But it'd be a little different if her Adolescence Syndrome was resolved."

"Because you had a similar case and you remember your trip to the future? In her case, it won't make a difference. Knowing her own future won't give her the means to save herself. There is no such thing. That's why she hasn't done it."

He knew Rio was right.

"This isn't like avoiding a traffic accident."

This was also true. But he couldn't let the hopelessness stop him. He had to find some hope somewhere.

"Futaba."

"……"

"Toyohama said she had a dream about Mai's accident. Do you think that's because Adolescence Syndrome sent me four days into the future? If so, that means memories might get shared with people other than the actual time traveler."

"And I'm saying that's just wishful thinking, Azusagawa."

"……"

Rio was staying firm on the matter. And he knew exactly why.

"I had a similar dream."

"……"

"After your Adolescence Syndrome was resolved...I dreamed I dragged you home with me. You were a wreck."

"So…"

"But even if you manage to send memories of today back to yourself three years ago, it won't change anything. It won't make a difference."

"Yeah, I'd probably just go, 'What a weird dream.'"

If he didn't know it affected him, it was easy to simply move on. Sakuta was well aware of that.

"Even if it bugged you, the core problem would be the exact same. Three years ago, you still had no way to save Shouko."

Not now, not then.

"Azusagawa, even if…" Her voice got grim. "Say a miracle happened. The past is forever changed and Shouko's condition gets cured. Is that actually what you want?"

Sakuta knew exactly what she was asking.

"Makinohara getting better is a good thing."

And that was precisely why he played dumb.

"You brought this up, so I'm sure you get it. You know what changing the past means."

She wasn't letting him off the hook.

"…Yeah."

"If fourth-grade Shouko overcomes her fears of the future and doesn't get Adolescence Syndrome…then big Shouko will never exist."

"I know that."

"You don't, Azusagawa."

Her voice was quiet, but there was a quiver in it. She was hoping he wouldn't understand.

"If big Shouko doesn't exist, you won't have met her on Shichirigahama Beach two years ago."

"Right."

"If you don't meet her there, then you don't try to emulate her."

"Mm."

"You don't take the Minegahara entrance test to chase after her."

"Yeah."

"You don't meet me or Kunimi."

"……Mm."

"You will never cross paths with Sakurajima."

Sakuta had already thought all of this through.

"Are you fine with that?"

"Of course not."

How could he be?

"A life where I don't meet Mai is no life at all."

"Then…"

"And let's be clear, I'm dead set against going through high school without you and Kunimi."

Or Tomoe and Nodoka. Meeting Shouko two years ago had made him who he was today. If that past changed, so would this future. Just as the Shouko who'd received his heart was no longer with them.

"That's why I've been pretending I hadn't figured this out, even though I had. Praying that somebody would save Makinohara for me."

"Azusagawa…"

"But that didn't work. You can't just leave these things to fate."

None of this was funny, but he laughed out loud anyway. It helped him banish his fears.

"You chose a future with Mai."

"I did. Then. I chose it without realizing this option existed. I thought I had to choose between getting in the accident and saving Makinohara, or avoiding the accident and living my life with Mai."

"And that's all ahead of you. You and Sakurajima are finally going to be happy. And you're just letting that slip away."

"Once I figured it out, it was all over. Now that I know there's still a chance…pretending I don't is too much."

"I thought you only picked fights you could win."

"Yep. I only want to fight when I can win."

"Says the man about to throw away everything that matters to him, everything he's built up for himself, on a chance so small it might not even exist. Do you even have the nerve to tell Mai any of this?"

"That's the real challenge! If she starts crying, I'm in trouble."

5

When he was done talking to Rio, Sakuta called Mai.

He told her about the call from Shouko's mother.

"Okay," she said. "I'll be right out. Wait downstairs."

And she hung up.

Sakuta told Kaede to guard the fort, and as promised, it was less than five minutes before Mai met him outside.

"Let's go," she said.

He nodded, and they started walking. He set a faster pace than usual, but Mai kept up just fine.

On the main road, they saw a bus bound for the hospital coming up from behind.

"Let's grab that."

They raced ahead to the bus stop and hopped on via the back doors. It was New Year's Eve. Businesses and schools were closed, so the bus was almost empty. The long seat at the very back was open, so the two of them sat down there.

The doors closed, and the bus driver turned the blinker on and slowly started pulling out.

As he did, Sakuta said, "Mai."

"Yes?"

"I still want to save Makinohara."

He spoke clearly, looking straight ahead. Keeping his voice low and quiet yet firm. Making sure she knew what he was thinking.

"Mm." Her voice was just as quiet. He could see her nod out of the corner of his eye. That was it. She wasn't surprised or upset. She didn't press him for more details or get flustered. She just said, "If you want to, you should."

"Mai…?"

He hadn't said anything yet. He hadn't told her there was anything to this besides a wish for a hope beyond hope. But it felt like she already knew everything.

"The future schedule in Shouko's room. She's the one who wrote and erased that, right? That must have happened when her Adolescence Syndrome first presented itself in fourth grade. And it's still active, right?"

He was definitely a little surprised she'd worked it all out. But it also explained why she was taking this in stride.

"So go ahead. Change the past."

Sakuta's hand was resting on the seat between them, and she laid her hand over his. The seat in front of them shielded them from any prying eyes.

"You've been crying every time I leave you alone."

"Only, like, every other day."

"You're such a liar."

He couldn't fool Mai. But the lie was worth telling. Acting tough had made her smile.

"Or will you change your mind if I grab you and don't let go?"

"It's hard to say no to you."

"Then I can't ask. I think you'd regret that choice the rest of your life."

"……"

"It's hard to go on living wondering if you could have made a difference."

"Mm."

"But I think that feeling would fade over time. You'd cry less often. Together, we could get past it."

"Yeah. That might not be so bad."

"But we made a promise. On Christmas Eve, in the green room at the TV station. That we'd be happy together."

"Yeah."

He'd never forget. Those words were what kept him going.

"So this is just the long way around."

"A bit, yeah."

"We just have to forget it all once and start over."

"Yeah. That's all."

"I'm going to meet you again."

"Mm."

"And fall in love once more."

"Right."

"You're going to ask me out again."

"I know I'll find you."

He squeezed her hand, taking in her warmth. Feeling her presence with the whole of his palm.

"And then we'll be happy together."

Mai looked at him and smiled.

"I promise."

He squeezed her hand again, tighter. Mai laughed a little like that had tickled her.

The bus reached the stop by the hospital.

They got off, still holding hands.

Inside, the usual nurse was waiting for them. Shouko was in the ICU, and you couldn't just waltz in and out of there—Shouko's mother must have arranged this.

"Go on, Sakuta."

"You're not coming?"

"The schedule's in her room. You'll need it, right?"

"Right."

If there was a key to resolving Shouko's Adolescence Syndrome, it would be that.

"Okay, Mai, you handle that."

They split up, and he followed the nurse.

The ICU was in the back of the building, normally off-limits to visitors. The hall had no patients and almost no doctors or nurses.

At the end of the deserted corridor was a pair of automatic doors. He was led into the visitor's changing room. Like on his previous visit, he donned a sort of smock and was given a hat that resembled what painters wear. Special slippers for his feet. He washed his hands with incredible thoroughness.

The nurse checked him over carefully and cleared him to proceed.

He was led through another door on the other side of the changing room. This still wasn't Shouko's ICU room—just a super-sterile corridor. There were glass windows along the right wall, allowing them to look into each room.

The nurse leading him stopped. Sakuta saw faces on the other side of the glass. Shouko's parents, dressed exactly like him. They bowed at the sight of him. He did the same.

A week before, he hadn't been allowed in the actual room. This time, it was different.

"Go on," the nurse said. So he stepped into the ICU.

There was a very distinct silence.

Only the hum of the medical devices disturbed the quiet. One sounded exactly like a fridge, while another seemed to be pumping something. And these mechanical noises just made the silence more pronounced. Like the devices were manufacturing stillness.

Shouko was lying on the bed, surrounded by these machines. Her eyes were closed.

"Shouko, Azusagawa's here," her mother said. There was a quiver in her voice.

Shouko's eyes opened halfway. At first, they just stared at the ceiling, but then they found her parents' faces.

"Makinohara," Sakuta said, unable to wait.

Her gaze wandered and finally locked onto him.

"Sakuta…"

Her voice was muffled by the oxygen mask. She lifted her little hand, reaching for him.

"Come closer," her mother said, stepping aside to let him in.

"Yeah, it's me."

He didn't know what else to say. His body moved without thinking, placing both his hands around hers. He didn't tighten his grip at all. Her hand felt so tiny, her fingers so thin—he got scared that if he held it too tight, it would melt away.

"I didn't want you to see me like this."

"Why not?"

"I mean, surrounded by machines…"

"It's kinda badass."

"Not a compliment girls really strive for."

But she cracked the smallest of smiles.

With her free hand, she pulled the mask off.

He glanced at the nurse to see if that was okay. She nodded.

Shouko put the mask down on the table positioned over her bed. On it were a junior high school textbook, a pencil box, and a pencil.

"You've been studying?"

"When I feel up to it. Now and then."

"We'll be just outside, Shouko," her mother said. She bowed with her eyes, and Shouko's parents and the nurse all left.

Sakuta and Shouko were alone.

"……"

He didn't know what to say at first. The regular rhythm of the machines and his own emotions were both overwhelming. He could feel the tension coiling around him. An invisible wave of fear was rising up from his soles.

"You kept your promise."

"Mm?"

"Mom said you came to see me every day."

"Some days I had to work."

Shouko laughed. She knew why he was joking.

"Thank you," she said.

"Makinohara."

"Yes?"

"There's something you should hear."

Part of him wasn't sure if he should tell her. But if he didn't now, he would never get another chance. That was how bad her condition was. Every part of this room was telling him as much. The looks on the faces of her family said it louder than words.

"It's about the future schedule you showed me."

"......"

"The one filled with things you didn't write."

"Sakuta," she said, looking away. At nothing in particular. Eyes focused beyond the ceiling. Maybe at the sky above. "I've been dreaming."

"You have?"

"Very strange dreams."

She spoke like she was lost in memories.

"I was in high school, and I met a younger you on the beach at Shichirigahama. And teased you a lot."

"......"

Shouko had taken control of the conversation, but Sakuta never considered stopping her. He knew exactly what she was talking about—those memories weren't easily forgotten.

"Then I dreamed I was in college, and I stayed at your house, cooked for you, cleaned, and gave Nasuno baths."

This was hardly a coincidence. Little Shouko's dreams of high school were dreams of the Shouko who was Sakuta's first love. And the college Shouko was the one who'd stayed with him from late November until Christmas Eve.

"Every morning, I woke up, said good morning to you…and saw you off at the front door."

"......"

"When you got home, I'd welcome you back with an apron on. Before bed, I'd say good night. And when morning came, we did it all over again. Like we were newlyweds. It was so much fun."

"Makinohara."

"Sometimes we went out together."

"That wasn't a dream."

"In a chapel with an ocean view, I tried on a wedding dress, and you looked so awkward, but I managed to get a few compliments out of you."

"It wasn't—"

"Even if it was just a dream, I loved spending time with you."

"All of that…really happened."

"It was so much fun."

Shouko smiled, looking completely content.

Her eyes had turned back to him. He could feel her gentle gaze.

"I know, Sakuta."

Her smile became a little impish. Like she was imitating her older self.

"Makinohara?"

"I know everything. I know that was a real future and that we're in the future now. I already know."

"Yeah, that's right. And if we change the past, maybe there's still a way to save you."

He knew it was a faint hope. The odds were next to nothing. He was painfully aware of that.

"But I can't," Shouko said. She slowly shook her head.

"Why not…?"

"I don't think a do-over will cure my condition."

"We don't know that. There must be *something*…"

"But if I go back in time, maybe I can save you from the grief you're feeling."

"What…?"

"I know everything."

"……"

"I'm making you suffer."

"No, you've done nothing wrong."

"I was so scared of the future that I got Adolescence Syndrome. And that's how I met you."

"And I owe you everything for that. I've never once regretted meeting either version of you. All the time we spent together matters. I wouldn't be who I am now if we hadn't met."

There was so much he wanted to tell her. He wanted to use every bit of strength he could muster and shout it from the rooftops. But now that he was face-to-face with her, Sakuta couldn't do any of that. He had to keep his voice down and remain calm.

"You did great, Sakuta."

"……"

"So it's okay."

There were tears forming in her eyes.

"Makinohara…?"

"I'll get the do-over right this time. I'll make a future where we never meet."

"What are you—?"

"So you can have a future where you don't have to be sad. Even if it means we never meet, if you're happy, then—"

"No, you can't— That's not what I meant to—"

Shouko's eyes were on the ceiling again, unfocused. It didn't seem like she could hear him. Her lips were barely moving, her voice almost inaudible.

Nothing Sakuta said was getting through to her at all.

"Don't do this, Makinohara!"

His words didn't reach her.

"The do-over should be for *you*."

His feelings didn't, either.

"You don't need to worry anymore, Sakuta."

"I'm not…"

"Just leave it all to me."

"No…"

"I promise I'll make you happy."

"You matter, too!"

Shouko's hand went limp.

"Makinohara…?"

"……"

She didn't answer. Didn't respond at all.

"H-help!" he called out.

The nurse stepped in quickly and checked Shouko's vitals.

"Don't worry. She's just asleep."

He couldn't *not* worry. There was an unsaid "for now" couched in that reassurance, and that hit him hard. He was a mess. Shouko had made up her mind, and what she'd said had rattled him to the core.

Sakuta had come here intending to save *her*. She'd been born with this awful condition, and he believed she deserved to be saved from her fate. He still did. But even now, she was only concerned about him. She'd said she wanted to save *him*.

"Do what's best for *you*, Makinohara," he croaked as he gradually lost control of his roiling emotions. "It's okay to put yourself first."

Fighting back the tears, shoulders shaking.

"Let's step outside a minute," the nurse suggested.

He followed her lead. There was nothing he could do here now. He'd just be in the way.

Outside the clean room, he stared back at Shouko once through the glass. She couldn't have been satisfied with her lot in life. She must have wanted more. But in her sleep, she smiled, like she was happy.

He couldn't stand looking at that contented expression. He quickly returned to the changing room. The smock and hat came off and went into the disposal bin.

"I'll call for you if anything happens," the nurse said.

He nodded without glancing back and went outside.

Back through the double doors.

Mai and Rio were waiting for him.

"Sakuta."

"Mai..."

"How's Shouko?"

"Asleep."

"Oh."

Mai lowered her eyes, biting her lip.

"Sakurajima, he should see it."

Rio was looking at the printout in Mai's hand.

"Here," Mai said, holding it up.

"......?!"

Surprise and doubt rushed over him.

"How…?"

The entries had been rewritten. Replacing the old version completely.

There was no junior high graduation. No high school.

It couldn't even be called a future schedule anymore.

Yet it was exactly right. Sakuta could never have written words like this, words that spoke directly to his heart.

All the fields were filled out.

"Thank you."

"Good job."

"I love you."

Live your life and treasure all three.

The handwriting wasn't always steady, but they were written with force.

Big Shouko's three favorite things to hear.

The three things he'd told little Shouko, in turn.

And at the very bottom…

I want to become a nicer person.

"…What the…?"

Something fell on the page. It seeped into the paper, blurring the words *Shouko Makinohara, Class 4-1.*

He knew it was his tears, but he couldn't stop them.

"Why…?"

"We spoke to Shouko's mother when she came out of the ICU. She said yesterday Shouko suddenly insisted she had to do her homework."

"What am I supposed to do?" he asked, desperately turning to Rio. "How am I supposed to help her?"

"……"

Rio just looked downcast, saying nothing.

"Makinohara…knew everything. About Shouko, about me… She

knew she had a chance at changing history. She knew all of that, and because she did…she said this time she'd make sure we never meet. She said that way, even if she was gone, I wouldn't have to grieve. And I don't—"

It had been his one hope. A faint possibility that could only be attained by going back in time. Yet Shouko was using that not for herself, but for Sakuta.

"Sorry, Azusagawa," Rio said, visibly upset. Her eyes met his. "I can only think of one thing to do."

She held out a pencil. A red one—like teachers use to grade papers.

"……?"

"Sakuta," Mai said. "Shouko worked hard on this."

She put her hand on his back.

"……"

"So you need to mark her homework complete."

"?!"

"Tell her what a good job she did."

"I…"

Fingers trembling, he reached for the pencil. He couldn't hold it right. But he gritted his teeth and forced his fingers to tighten around it. His tears would have to wait for a moment.

He put the printout down on a low table by a bench in the hall.

He didn't hesitate further.

Conscious of the heat behind his eyes, Sakuta smiled and drew a big flower. Going for the biggest flower mark any homework had ever seen. It covered the whole damn page, like a midsummer sunflower.

When he was done, he looked up and found Mai crying. Rio was crying, too. Crying like a sun-shower, beaming all the while.

Bells rang out, marking the arrival of the New Year.

They'd been granted permission to stay the night at the hospital.

They were in the hall just outside the ICU. On a bench against the wall, wrapped in blankets, waiting.

Shouko's parents had said they could use Shouko's room in the main wing, but they'd decided to stay closer to her.

The nurse had brought the blankets, saying they looked cold.

Sakuta and Mai were wrapped in the same blanket, huddled together. Rio was on a seat nearby. Yuuma was with her, having shown up later on.

None of them spoke. They just sat in silence.

"A new year," Yuuma whispered. In the darkened hallway, the light of his phone's screen seemed very bright.

Nobody felt like calling the New Year "happy."

Nobody here was in the mood to celebrate.

Time was about to rob Shouko of her life, and the hall was filled with silent prayers for time to stand still.

But in time, the tolling of the bells at the nearby temples faded.

The hospital corridor was silent once more. The only noise came when one of them shifted in their seat.

Sakuta and Mai were sitting shoulder to shoulder, and he could hear her breathing.

At some point, it had grown rhythmic. Soft.

Her eyes were closed, her weight resting against him.

He looked over, and Rio was asleep with her hands around her knees. Yuuma, too, had his head down and was sound asleep.

The sky outside the window was getting brighter.

Morning was almost here.

The first morn of the new year.

Sakuta said a prayer to the unrisen sun, hoping that Shouko would be okay.

And that was the last thought he had before his consciousness faded.

He thought he heard the click of the ICU doors opening.

"Shouko has..."

He thought he heard someone speaking.

But his mind was off in the world of slumber before either sound could reach him.

He dreamed—
Of a classroom he'd never seen.
Little desks in rows.
An elementary school.
The kids looked maybe third or fourth grade.
All facing their desks.
Writing something on a printout.
Sakuta recognized one of the girls.
An extra-small one, sitting bolt upright in her chair.
Absorbed in her writing.
Her expression serious but excited.
He tried to remember her name, but it escaped him.
He felt like he *should* know it, but racking his mind got him nowhere.
"All done!" a boy in the middle said, throwing up his hand.
"Me too!"
"Same here!"
Hands were going up all around.
As the rest of the class got noisy, the girl kept writing. Everyone else was done and goofing off, but she kept going.
The teacher came over to her.
She knelt down beside the girl.
"Just write as far as you feel comfortable," she said.
The girl looked up a moment later.
With a proud smile.
She held out the page with both hands.
"All done!" she said.
And gave her teacher a bright smile.

Chapter
4

kindness, and a hand offered in kind

1

Someone was shaking him.

He was lying facedown, and someone had their hands on his back.

Oh, is it morning?

As his mind woke up…

"Get up, Sakuta!" His sister's voice.

He half opened his eyes and reached for the clock by the bed. As he did, winter's chill prickled his skin. Leaving the comforter's warmth seemed like an insurmountable task. He felt like staying in bed the rest of his life.

It was eight.

The temperature in the room was fifty-nine degrees.

It was January 6.

"It's still winter vacation, Kaede."

It was the last day of break. Third term started tomorrow. He pulled his hand back under the covers, wrapping himself up like the filling of a chocolate cornet.

"You're the one who's got a shift at nine."

"Oh. You'll have to cover for me, Kaede."

"Wow. There'll be so much egg on your face later. You send your sister to work for you and you'll never hear the end of it."

"Okay."

"Okay how?"

"I can handle that, no prob."

"Well I can't! Get up and go!"

She gave him a stronger shake.

"No! I'm still asleep."

"You clearly aren't!"

"How'd you know?"

Obviously, all this talking had been a dead giveaway.

It was no use. He sat up. His eyes met Kaede's. Her school was also on vacation, but she was in uniform.

"I'm getting used to seeing you in that."

"Y-yeah?"

Trouble with bullies at her old school had left Kaede not attending classes for a long time, but with third term of her third year quickly approaching, she finally felt ready to try again.

Over vacation, Sakuta had been helping her practice, and they were getting solid results. Yesterday she'd gone all the way to her school's gates and back on her own.

Last night she'd been excited to do it again.

"You're gonna do your practice run now?"

"I already did it."

"Whoa."

"Mm-hmm."

"You make it there okay?"

"Mm…it's still pretty stressful, but…"

He could tell she was putting on a brave face, but Kaede's smile looked genuine. She was clearly proud of herself.

"I'm glad you've grown so independent."

"I—I always have been!" she protested.

"Like, a week ago, you only made it to school plastered to my back."

"Th-that was ages ago! Ancient history."

She *hmphed* once and turned away. Her body language was still pretty childish. And to top it off, her stomach growled.

"Breakfast?"

"Not yet."

"Figured."

"Well, you were sleeping!"

That made it sound like this was *his* fault. She hadn't been running around on an empty stomach because of a weird "I want to eat breakfast with you, Sakuta" thing; she was just literally unable to cook at all and even slapping together a simple breakfast was beyond her.

"Definitely not very independent," he muttered to no one in particular.

"I'm hungry! C'mon!" Kaede said, yanking his arm while pretending she hadn't heard him.

He made it off the bed and headed to the kitchen to make his sister some breakfast.

"Thanks for the food!"

On the table was toast (fresh from the toaster), ham and eggs, and sausages (fresh from the skillet) with a few chopped tomatoes and some shredded lettuce.

Not one thing about this menu was the least bit difficult. Kaede could easily learn to do it herself.

"That was pretty good."

"Glad you liked it."

They wolfed down the food, and then he washed the dishes.

Then he splashed some water on his face, brushed his teeth, fixed his bed head—kinda—and got dressed.

"I'm off to work."

"Bye!"

Kaede saw him off as he left the apartment.

He took the elevator to the first floor. In the street outside, he ran into a familiar face.

"Oh, Sakuta!"

A high school girl who wore her sparkly blond hair in a side ponytail was coming out of the building opposite. Even at this hour, her makeup was a wonder to behold.

"Mornin'," she said. Her name was Nodoka Toyohama. She was dragging a little suitcase behind her.

"Morning. Bye." He waved and started walking toward the station. The restaurant he worked at was in that area.

"Er, hey! Wait up!"

Nodoka hurried after him, suitcase rattling. Her boots also made quite a racket.

"Why'd you rush off?"

"Not like we had plans."

"Sure, but if you bump into someone you know, it's normal to walk together! We're both headed to the station. Also, why are you up and about this early? It's still winter vacation."

It was too early for this much conversation.

"That's why I took more shifts." He gave her a sidelong glance. "You running away from home?"

Between the hair, the makeup, and the suitcase, she sure *looked* like a runaway. Exactly the kinda girl they showed in alarmist news segments about schoolgirls who stayed out all night.

"Already did that."

"Right, I remember now."

Nodoka had already ditched her home over disagreements with her mother. Now she lived with Mai, her sister (from a different mother). This had all happened three months ago, in the fall.

She was trotting a bit to keep up with him. That made her suitcase rattle even louder.

"Lemme carry that for you," he said, reaching for it.

"Oh, sure." Nodoka initially blinked at the offer but quickly let him take it. "Thanks."

She didn't look like the type to willingly accept help, which made it always feel novel when she did.

"What's in it?"

It wasn't very heavy.

"We've got a mini gig in a mall in Saitama."

So presumably this was stuff she needed during the show. There was a reason for her slightly outlandish look—she was in show business, specifically as a member of an idol group named Sweet Bullet.

On weekends, she was always off somewhere, throwing herself into concerts. Listening to her chatter about that, they headed to the station together.

It was still rush hour, and Fujisawa Station was packed with suits. People going in, people coming out, people switching trains.

Sakuta stopped by the JR gates.

"Have a good show," he said as he handed the suitcase back to Nodoka.

"Mm, thanks. Oh, right…"

He'd taken a step toward work, but she stopped him.

"Mm?"

"You should come to our Valentine's show next month."

"Why?"

"I've got a center number."

"So?"

"And afterward you can ask for chocolate directly from any one of us."

"Okay, so I can get one from the girl who doesn't wear panties?"

He'd gone to a show of theirs once before, and the group leader had yelled, "Idols don't wear panties!" Her name was Uzuki Hirokawa. He'd forgotten the rest of their names, but that line had left an impression, so he remembered hers. Also, she had a slim model build that kinda resembled Mai's, which had helped.

"Why not me?!"

"You're legally obligated to give me chocolate anyway."

"Huh?"

"As my sister-in-*law*."

"That's ridiculous. And we aren't in-laws yet."

"It's gonna happen, so you might as well get used to it."

"You're awfully sure my sister won't dump you, huh?"

"I refuse to even consider the possibility."

Nodoka sighed dramatically.

"Fine. She promised she'd come, so…"

"Then I'll be there, too."

"It's a full-size arena. Six thousand five hundred yen."

"You're gonna charge me? Don't you have tickets for family?"

That was a lot of money for him.

"You oughtta fork up that much for you sister-in-law's big day, Bro."

"……"

"……"

She'd said that last word to tease him, but when he stared back at her without saying a word, she turned bright red. Not just her ears and neck, either. She was probably scalding hot all the way to her toes.

"Quit gawking! Bye!" she snapped, before dashing through the gate. He watched her flee, considering this his responsibility as her future in-law.

"Being a brother-in-law might not be so bad…," he muttered.

2

"Good morning."

The restaurant wasn't open yet. The lights on the floor were still out, and the heat had only just been turned on—so it was barely better than being outside.

He ducked behind the lockers to change into his uniform.

This corner of the break room doubled as the men's changing area.

As he stepped in, a tall boy stepped out—having just finished changing.

"'Sup."

Their eyes met. This was a friend of his from school, Yuuma Kunimi.

"Yo." Sakuta took his turn in the shadows. "So cold," he grumbled, changing as fast as possible.

"Don't see you on morning shifts often, Sakuta."

"Same goes for you. No practice?"

"Morning practice is at noon today."

"You're working a shift before you go do club stuff? Have you lost it?"

"It's Kamisato's birthday next month."

Saki Kamisato was Yuuma's girlfriend. She was in the same class as Sakuta and really had it in for him.

"How much you gonna pour into that?"

"That's not fair. I'm not buying anything *that* expensive."

"It's the feelings that matter."

"Says the man who didn't even learn Sakurajima's birthday until the day in question," Yuuma cackled. "And she was filming in Kanazawa, so you took a Shinkansen all the way out there just to say, 'Happy birthday!' You're way crazier than I am."

Yuuma was having a good laugh about it, but none of that had been funny for Sakuta at the time.

"You said you had to borrow money for a return ticket from her? How much does it cost to Kanazawa and back?"

"Thirty thousand round trip. Plus the hotel…"

"So you've been spending way more."

"The memories are priceless."

"The expenses are real."

"That's why I'm on a morning shift."

He stepped out from behind the lockers, tugging his apron strings.

"Then let's break a leg."

Yuuma got off his stool, punched his and Sakuta's time cards, and left the break room. Sakuta followed.

Paying back his debt to Mai would take the bulk of his vacation wages.

"Just promise you won't end up a gigolo, Sakuta."

"Is a househusband acceptable?"

"You'll have to check with Sakurajima on that."

"Will do."

*   *   *

It was noon, start of the lunch rush. Yuuma had wrapped up his shift and gone off to basketball practice.

"The rest is all yours!"

"Heartless bastard!"

He was replaced by a student a year below them at school, Tomoe Koga. A petite girl, only five feet tall. She wore her hair in a fashionably short, fluffy bob, with cute makeup to complete the look. She finished changing into her uniform and joined him on the floor.

"Oh? You've been here all morning, senpai?" she asked the moment she spotted him.

"You're rolling in late? The nerve."

"This is my shift!"

"……"

"Wh-what? Something on my face?"

"Nah, it's just…"

"Just what?"

"Hmm, best not to say."

"Huh?"

"I mean, if I do, you'll one-hundred percent accuse me of having no tact, so I'll just think it."

"Thinking tactless stuff is also bad!"

"In that case, might as well say it. Koga, has your face swollen up?"

"Ugh, I was afraid of that!"

She tried to hide her face with her hands.

"All that New Year's mochi gave you mochi-soft cheeks, eh?"

"You're the worst! You're terribad! Don't look!"

"First a peach butt, now mochi cheeks! Your girl power's skyrocketing!"

"I'm gonna lose the weight! And when I do, you'd better say sorry!"

She puffed up her cheeks in protest but then realized that made her look even rounder, so she quickly deflated.

"That happens, I'll buy you a cheeseburger."

"I don't need more calories! I need respect!"

"Then I promise I'll eat your cheeseburger for you. You get to watch."

"Just imagining that is infuriating, so I'll eat the damn cheeseburger."

"So how many pounds you gotta lose to make this happen?"

"Uh...well, I'm eighty— Don't make me say that aloud!"

"I won't tell a soul."

"You're the soul I don't want knowing! We're on the clock—do your job!"

"Sure, sure. Quit dieting and take some orders."

"I'm not dieting *now*!"

Fuming, she stalked off toward a waiting table. By the time she got there, she was wearing a professional smile.

"Kids are so restless these days."

Sakuta figured he should probably focus himself. He spotted another customer who had just come in.

"Welcome!" he said, grabbing a menu and heading over.

He quickly realized he knew her.

It was another friend of his, Rio Futaba. It was winter vacation, but she was in their school uniform anyway.

"Not often you come here, Futaba. Kunimi's already gone."

"Practice, right? I passed him at the station."

"So you were at school experimenting?"

Rio was in the Science Club and had the distinction of being the sole member. Which meant she had to show real results. She spent a great deal of time doing experiments to meet those expectations.

He led her to a table.

"Please hit the button when you're ready to order," he said. Very by the book. He took a step away.

"Wait, I'm ready."

"Go ahead."

He took his order pad out of his apron pocket.

"The carbonara," Rio said, pointing at the top picture on the pasta page.

"Okay, one carbonara."

"...No, sorry, let's go with this one."

She pointed at a veggie-heavy tomato sauce.

"Ah yes, the one with two hundred fewer calories, of course."

"......"

His statement had been entirely accurate, but it earned him a frosty glare.

"Is there a diet craze running through the female population?"

He'd just been talking about this with Tomoe.

"Almost certainly. Always is, post-holidays."

"You look just like you did before vacation."

He certainly couldn't see a visible difference.

"It's the places you can't see...," she muttered.

"Oh, I get you."

Sakuta's eyes drifted to her blazer. It *did* look a bit tighter. Her blouse was definitely struggling to contain everything underneath.

Rio wasn't much taller than Tomoe, but her bust scored a clear victory. Tomoe didn't really have much in that department.

"The world is not fair."

As he despondently stared at Rio's chest, he realized she had her phone out and was taking a picture of him.

"Ma'am, we ask that patrons refrain from taking photos in the restaurant."

"This is evidence."

"Of what?"

"Of you ogling me. For the report I'll file with Sakurajima."

"Uh, Futaba."

"What?"

"I've got a date with Mai after this shift."

"So?"

"I'll get scolded, so...keep this between us?"

"That smirk on your face suggests you'd rather I tell her."

"I do love Mai's scoldings."

"That's why you're a rascal."

Rio sighed, then gave up and put her phone away.

3

As scheduled, Sakuta worked his butt off until two, then quickly got changed. He was out of there at 2:05.

"I'm off."

"Oh, okay senpai! Have a good one!"

Like he'd told Rio, he had a fun date planned with Mai.

It was a bit late for a New Year's shrine visit, but they were gonna do it anyway.

He walked right past the JR gates Nodoka had taken that morning, moving to the south side of Fujisawa Station.

He crossed a connecting bridge and was about to turn into the Enoden station when something made him pause.

It was a group of junior high kids doing a fund drive.

He stood still a minute, listening to see what cause this was for. He soon figured out it was to help poor children in developing countries get a proper education.

Sakuta took all the coins out of his wallet.

"Here," he said, dropping them into the box the nearest boy was holding. The coins rattled as they fell. Probably three hundred yen, total.

"Thank you!"

The boy's voice was so loud, Sakuta cringed and quickly fled the scene. The last thing he wanted was for people to think he was doing it for the attention. He went past an Odakyu department store and into the Enoden Fujisawa Station, running his train pass through the gates.

A train bound for Kamakura was just coming in.

This was the start of the line, so the tracks stopped at the end of the platform.

He went around the left side of the green-and-cream train and took a seat. He was alone in the car.

When the departure time arrived, the train slowly pulled out of the station.

The train dawdled along, feeling like it was still getting up to speed. But before it did, it started slowing down to stop at Ishigami Station. From there, it headed south, stopping at Yanagikoji, Kugenuma, and Shonankaigankoen on the way to Enoshima Station.

Next, the tracks turned east toward Kamakura, following the coast. Once it passed Koshigoe, it emerged from the rows of houses and provided an unobstructed view of the water. The clear winter skies, the deep ocean blue—a soothing beauty exclusive to this time of year.

Sakuta watched it roll by until the train reached Kamakura Station—end of the line.

He got out and left the gates.

"Sakuta," a voice called.

Mai was standing by the ticket machines. She had her hair in braids and a pair of fake glasses on—a disguise. But her makeup was flawless, so she was still attracting plenty of attention.

She must have noticed him studying her appearance.

"Just to be clear, this isn't for you. It's left over from the shoot."

"Aw. Even if it isn't for me, you could have lied and said it was."

"You should be happy I didn't bother removing it."

"Was *that* for me?"

"So what do you have to say?"

"Mai, you're supercute. I love you."

She smiled, clearly satisfied. This made him love her all the more.

"Come on," she said, taking his hand.

They walked off together.

Mai and Sakuta were visiting Tsurugaoka Hachimangu, a ten-minute walk from the station. On New Year's Day, this shrine would be so packed even grown-ups could get lost in the crowds. Even on the third day, the staff had to police the crowd size.

Mai showing up at a place like that would only invite disaster, so they'd waited until the sixth to make their visit out of an abundance of caution.

They walked through the torii gate and along the broad gravel path. After a bit, they reached the handwashing basin and cleaned their left hands, followed by their right. Then took a sip of the water from their right hand. Finally, they tipped the scoop backward, letting water run over the handle.

Sakuta hadn't planned on being so formal about it, but Mai insisted they do it right.

"You know a lot about this stuff, Mai?"

"Learned it for a role."

Mai told him about that job as they headed in. There was a towering staircase ahead, and the main shrine building was at the top.

They took it one step at a time.

At the top, Sakuta pulled out his wallet to drop a coin in.

"Ack…"

The coin pouch was empty.

"What?"

"Mai, can I borrow a coin?"

"Huh?" She blinked at him.

"I donated mine at Fujisawa Station."

"Oh…" She realized what had happened. "I don't want to begrudge you your hobbies, but…"

Despite this grumbling, she opened her wallet without a trace of resentment.

"Not exactly the word I'd use," he said.

It was just a thing he did.

The first one had been for research on a tricky medical condition. Maybe three years ago? Ever since, he'd been emptying his change into any donation box he saw. Even now he wasn't exactly sure why.

"Who was it who found himself without lunch money the other day?"

"But I got to eat half of yours, so I call that a win. You even did the 'Say *ahh!*' thing! My karma is finally paying off."

"I knew you'd say that. Wait."

"What?"

"Sakuta, do you have any paper money?"

"Yeah, a thousand-yen note."

He wasn't showing up to a date with just a handful of coins. But it was only a single bill…

He pulled it from his wallet to show her.

She promptly reached out and took it from him.

"Ack! Mai!"

But she was already headed toward the shrine.

"Look, you had money for an offering after all!"

She stopped by the collection box, muttering, "We're supposed to put bills in envelopes…"

And then dropped his one thousand yen in.

"Aughh!"

He let out a shriek, but Mai just bowed twice, clapped twice, and bowed again.

"You too."

No use crying over lost money. He stood next to Mai and put his hands together.

"……"

He made a proper report to the gods. And he followed it up with his usual request.

Once the unexpectedly expensive prayer was complete, they walked past the booths selling good luck charms and down the side staircase.

"Did you make a request worth the money?"

"I made sure to tell the gods I'd make you happy."

"You what?" she said, laughing.

"Then I asked them if we could have fewer crazy things happen this year."

"There were a lot…but that's also what brought us together."

"I've met enough wild bunny girls for one lifetime."

He'd met Mai at the library last spring. And before summer even arrived, he'd gotten mixed up in the petite devil's mess, been caught between two Rios over summer vacation, and when second term started had to deal with Mai and Nodoka swapping bodies. Then when fall was wrapping up, his sister got her memories back, becoming her old self again.

That was a lot for a single year, so he was hoping this one would take it easy on him.

"Also, since I'm broke now, I requested that you come over and cook dinner for me."

He said this in a very hammed-up voice, pointedly glancing at her.

"Fine. I'll come over."

"Great!"

"What do you want?"

"Those hamburg steaks of yours."

"If you help me make the patties."

"That would make it *my* hamburg steaks."

"Don't sweat the small stuff."

"But it makes a huge difference!"

On the way back from the shrine, they took a train from Kamakura Station but got off halfway, at Shichirigahama Station.

A small station on a single-track line. They ran their passes through the simple gate and went down a few stairs, and they were on the road outside the station.

They crossed a little bridge, and on the left stood their school, Minegahara High. Third term would start tomorrow. They'd have to come here every day.

But Sakuta put that depressing thought out of his mind and walked in the opposite direction, down the gentle slope toward the vast expanse of the ocean.

The light on Route 134 took forever, but they eventually crossed it. On the other side, they went down the stairs to the beach. The sun was already setting.

He and Mai walked along the surf, the sand catching their feet.

The sea breeze was chilly in winter. The roar of the surf drowned out all other sounds.

There were people here and there, but for the most part, they had the place to themselves. That was why he liked coming here.

"You really love the ocean, huh?" Mai asked.

"Not as much as I love you."

He hoped that would get him a reward, but she seemed disinclined. Actually, she seemed a little grumpy. He soon learned why.

"As much as this girl in your dreams?"

There was a challenge in her voice. She was feigning disinterest.

"Like I said before, nothing like *that*. I just feel like she helped me out."

"Yet you came here on dates."

"Only in dreams."

Which meant it was all very hazy. The specifics were hard to remember exactly.

Sakuta didn't even know her name.

Or have a clear idea what she looked like.

It was a dream, so what they'd talked about and what her voice sounded like eluded him.

But the general idea that she'd saved him stuck.

The same thing had happened two years back. Kaede's bullying had hit its peak, and the girl in his dreams had given him the courage to move forward.

He'd realized the uniform she wore was from Minegahara High— so when he and his sister had to move into a place of their own, he'd chosen to come here.

With a faint hope he might find her.

He hadn't.

He didn't meet any students who seemed like the one.

"Hmm," Mai grumbled.

"But you like it here, too," he said. The odds were stacked against him, but he was trying to change the subject.

"I dunno about that. I just have history with it."

"That movie was a huge hit."

This was a movie she'd made back in junior high.

It was set near Shichirigahama, and they'd filmed scenes on this very beach. Mai had played a girl born with a serious heart condition. A heart transplant was her only shot at life. Except no donor appeared to save her. A little girl struggling to make the most of her tragically short life—the entire country had wept for her. That girl had known the value of life better than anyone, and that depiction had received rave reviews abroad, earning the film major international awards.

And because of that film, awareness about the lead character's condition had skyrocketed. It had changed attitudes toward organ donation. For the better.

Sakuta had a green donor card in his pocket.

"It's cold. Let's go home."

Without waiting for an answer, Mai headed away from the water. Sakuta quickly caught up and took her hand.

"Your hands are cold," she said.

"That's why I'm making you warm them."

"It's usually the other way around."

She rolled her eyes at him but didn't try to shake him off. Instead, she grinned and tried to jam both their hands into his jacket pocket. That made him laugh.

As they goofed around, they reached the stairs leading up to the road, passing a family as they did.

The parents looked to be in their late thirties. Very close-knit.

And between them was a junior high school girl. She was talking to her parents, all smiles. Her smile so bright it really caught Sakuta's eye.

She ran off toward the surf, and her father called after her.

"But only for a little bit! I don't want you straining yourself!"

"Yes, I know you've had your operation, but…"

Before her mother finished, the girl called back, "I'm all better now! It'll be fine!"

She turned and waved at them.

Sakuta stopped in his tracks.

"Sakuta?" Mai frowned, leaning in.

"That girl...," he croaked.

He felt like he knew the girl running along the surf.

Laughing as she ran from the incoming wave.

Delighted to be alive.

Her long hair streaming behind her.

He tried to remember, but nothing came to mind.

Not her name.

Not where they'd met.

Nothing at all.

Thinking harder didn't reward him with an answer. There was nothing for him to find.

"...Never mind," he said, and he took a step up the stairs with Mai.

Then...

...his body moved with a will of its own.

His heart jumped ahead of his thoughts.

He turned toward the water and yelled a name he'd never heard.

"Makinohara!"

Loud enough to be heard above the roar of the waves.

The wind caught it, carrying it far.

And as he called the name, he remembered.

The name that taught him kindness.

Every precious memory came back to him, and he felt a heat behind his eyes.

"......"

The girl looked very surprised.

She turned back toward him, like she couldn't believe it.

Then a moment later, her face crumbled. She didn't even bother trying to wipe away the tears.

"That's right, Sakuta!" Shouko said with a smile.

afterword

If we count from when I drew up the initial plans, I've been working on this series for three years now.

I don't know how long it will run, but if you choose to keep reading the story of Sakuta and Mai, that would please me to no end.

Hajime Kamoshida

The end of a year Sakuta will never forget.

The next volume will bring new developments!

May: Found Mai.

June: Became Tomoe's fake boyfriend.

August: Proved he and Rio are real friends.

September: Watched Nodoka grow.

October: Accepted Kaede's decision.

December: Believed in Shouko's future.

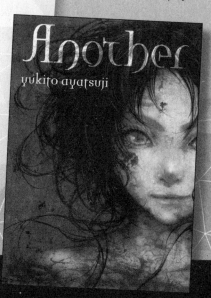